ST. JOHNS RIVER MONSTER

BY ARMAND ROSAMILIA

SEVEREDPRESS

ST. JOHNS RIVER MONSTER

Copyright © 2023 by Armand Rosamilia

WWW.SEVEREDPRESS.COM

ISBN: 978-1-922861-89-4

CHAPTER ONE

May 1975 - 10 a.m.

Brenda spotted it first, a thin pink skimming the surface for a few seconds. When the others turned to see what she was calling out, it was either gone or Brenda was mistaken.

Charlie and Dorothy both exchanged a glance, smiling. The couple had gotten the group of five friends together to go out fishing today. Maybe after so many hours out, between Jacksonville and the Atlantic Ocean, Brenda was getting bored.

"Are you messing with us?" Wallace asked Brenda with a grin.

Brenda was still staring out, her fishing pole dropped to the bottom of the boat. "Yeah, I saw it."

"Saw what, though? Likely a fish jumping, teasing me, since I haven't caught one all morning," Ed said and laughed. He opened another soda can and chugged it down. "How much longer are we going to be out here, anyway?"

"That's up to you all," Dorothy said. "You let me and Charlie know when you want to get back to shore." She glanced at Ed. "Unlike someone else, I've already caught too many fish to eat. Maybe I can take pity on your bad fishing skills and give you a couple of mine."

Ed laughed again. "Hey, I'll take 'em. It'll be good eatin' while I watch the Music City 420 on TV. Walltrip is winning it. I can feel it. His week."

Brenda ignored her friends, still watching the water. She had seen something and it was big. Not a fish, not a gator, nothing she'd ever seen before. She was raised on the water like the others. They all thought they'd seen it all, but Brenda knew better now.

After a few more minutes she guessed it had either disappeared or moved on. Brenda knew what she'd seen, though.

She picked up her fishing pole and cast it out, right where she'd seen the creature. Maybe she could catch it and show the others she wasn't seeing things.

Ed was still without so much as a bite and Brenda smiled when he groaned as Dorothy hooked another sea trout and pulled it onto the boat.

They all started to make fun of Ed but Brenda glanced over Dorothy's shoulder and saw the ripple on the surface and a hint of pink, right where Dorothy's line had been.

"There. See it? There," Brenda shouted and stood, nearly capsizing the boat.

"Sit down," Charlie shouted. "All I see is the storm clouds heading our way. Everyone wrap this up so we can race the thunder and lightning to shore."

Brenda was still watching the water. She'd seen it again.

The important thing for the rest of her friends was the impending storm, which was bearing down on them out of nowhere. A typical Florida May thunderstorm was going to drop on them out of nowhere, with thunder and lightning and buckets of rain.

Being on the ocean during a raging storm was not the best place to be.

The boat was turned toward the safety of the shore.

Brenda kept looking at the water but now all she saw were the first fat raindrops beginning to fall.

"I hate getting wet," Ed groaned.

Dorothy laughed. "And yet, here we are surrounded by water."

Ed looked up. "I mean, I hate it when I get soaked from rain." He sighed. "Why am I even answering you, huh?"

"That's on you, fool," Dorothy said and laughed again.

Brenda was starting to relax. It wasn't anything dangerous in the ocean. She shook her head. It was a giant fish. Maybe a dolphin or a small whale? The pink coloring might only be a reflection of the sunlight before the clouds appeared so thickly.

"Who's coming to my place to watch Nascar?" Ed asked. "If you're coming, bring some of your darn fish."

Dorothy nodded. "I have more than enough, Ed. I will share."

"Excellent. I'm not too proud to beg. I have enough beer to drown all of us." Ed looked at Brenda. "Are you coming?"

She shook her head. "Watching cars go around in a circle for three hours? Nah. Not interested. I think I need a hot shower and a nap." Brenda glanced up at the sky as more rain fell now. "Nice day to get into my pajamas and curl up with a good book."

Wallace nodded in agreement. "I just started to read *Jaws*. Really good so far."

"I don't know what that is," Brenda admitted.

Wallace looked excited. "It's about a shark attacking an island."

Brenda groaned. "Maybe we should talk about something else while we're out here." She glanced at the surface of the ocean, now deluged by a steady pounding of rain.

Something was just under the surface, coming at them. She saw a glimmer of pink before it dove deeper.

Brenda pointed but then something hit the bottom of the boat and everyone grabbed the sides and gasped.

"I saw it again," Brenda said. She turned to Charlie. "Can't you go faster?"

Charlie sped up the boat as everyone held onto whatever they could.

Brenda closed her eyes. She didn't want to see the creature anymore. She knew it was real. Whatever it was, it was going to attack them. Dump them into the ocean and eat them.

Dorothy was whimpering. "I just saw it, too."

"I'm going as fast as I can," Charlie yelled, his voice cracking. "Not too far now. Maybe when we hit the shallows it will leave us alone."

Brenda knew they'd never make it. She could feel it.

The boat was bumped again and everyone screamed.

Brenda snapped her eyes open when it felt like the boat was being lifted from the water.

The rain was heavy now, nearly a blanket of water falling on her.

She wiped the rain from her hair and eyes.

The pink skin of the creature reared up next to the boat. A small head on a long, bony neck. It had ridges down the neck but she couldn't see the bulk of the creature still underwater.

"Like a dragon," Brenda whispered.

"Almost there," Charlie shouted.

The creature ducked under the surface again.

Brenda closed her eyes. *Maybe we'll make it,* she thought. *We'll have a crazy story to tell everyone. No one will believe it.*

The next bump of the boat lifted it, turning it sideways, as if they were on the back of the monster. Brenda felt bile rise in her throat, followed by salt water when the boat was tossed upside down into the ocean and she went under.

It was huge, moving swiftly through the water.

The pink creature bit into Wallace and Brenda wanted to scream but she couldn't, trying to figure out in her panic which way was up.

Brenda couldn't see with all of the blood in the water.

CHAPTER TWO

Present Day - 8 a.m.

This was going to be a nightmare, and Red Gandell knew it. He stood off to the side at the Jacksonville Airport, watching for the politician to exit so he could help him with his bags, take him to the nearby hotel and await his next orders.

Red had been working for News 4 the last three years, first as a gopher and the last year as a cameraman for their live events. This was going to be a live event like no other, he supposed.

A lot of pomp and backslapping nothing, Red thought.

The Florida governor was flying down from Tallahassee to give one of his big, fake smiles, shaking hands with the Jacksonville mayor, while they posed in front of the water.

New ground was being broken on the waterfront, as an old decrepit set of buildings had finally been ordered to be torn down, clearing a gorgeous view of the St. Johns River.

Of course, this live press conference was going to be all about the big, secret announcement everyone already knew: the guy who owned the nearby football team had already purchased the sixteen acres and was planning on building retail shops, a hotel and two sets of apartment buildings, all with a great view of the water.

Again, blocking the view for anyone downtown who happened by. Real estate was at a premium these days, and Red knew this new set of buildings would rake in millions of dollars.

It would also further congest the downtown area.

Red knew enough about the area, since he'd been born and raised in Jacksonville, and knew they'd bring up the same drivel they always brought up, to make the politicians look like they understood the history of the area.

The St. Johns River was a lazy river, with a very slow flow, and it is over three hundred miles long. Flows through or borders a dozen counties in Florida. The river flows north, like the Nile, but the politicians will erroneously say they are the only two rivers that flow north, which is incorrect. We don't know the exact number of rivers that actually flow north, but they are the main two always mentioned, Red thought.

He'd heard it all before. As a kid he was on the river a lot. He'd take a rowboat out or a canoe, they'd go fishing and swimming in the St. Johns

River. He'd kissed his first girl on the banks of it, too, and had his first beer.

Red had also been burnt by the sun while on the water far too many times to count. As a light-skinned redhead, he was prone to tan quickly and burn even quicker. Not that he cared while it was happening, because he loved to be outside. Even now, as an adult, there was nothing better than being in his yard working the grill or taking a nap on his open porch. A good day off was a day at the beach or riding his Jeep with the top down, checking out the ladies at Jacksonville Beach in their bikinis.

He knew he had a great life, although it was missing a few things, like a woman to share it all with. A better job, too, one that didn't slip from being a cameraman back to being a gopher.

"News 4? Is that you?"

Red turned to see an older woman with a sour puss on her face, wearing a gray suit.

"It is," Red said. He was wearing a News 4 t-shirt. He looked past the woman. "Where's the governor?"

"He'll be along shortly. I wanted to screen you first," she said.

Red smiled. "Are you going to frisk me or something?"

"No. He is." She stepped aside and a huge man, also wearing a suit, stepped up and began patting Red down.

This is ridiculous, Red thought. He looked around and frowned when everyone else in the airport watched and likely assumed he was dangerous. Red knew any one of them could be armed and ready to kill the governor, since he wasn't very well-liked. His recent battles with the largest employer in Florida as well as his stupid book-banning had really tanked his popularity.

Not that it mattered, because everyone knew he was going to announce a run for presidency within the next few weeks. This trip to Jacksonville was for good publicity. Red figured it was also to have a meeting with the owner of the property and the football team so he could get his vote as the governor took the next step in his political career. All the way to Washington D.C.

Red waited patiently as the governor, flanked by two more big goons, walked slowly, smiling and waving and shaking a hand here and there, all timed to offer the best shots of him. Even though there were no cameras following, except the occasional idiot with his cell phone out.

The woman nodded at Red. "This is our driver, sir. Ready when you are."

The governor smiled, his teeth white and perfect. He was staring past Red when he offered a hand and Red felt obligated to shake it.

A dead fish handshake, Red thought. *This guy is an even bigger idiot than I realized.*

Red led the group out of the airport and to the waiting limo, parked illegally outside. Not that anyone was going to tow it. Everyone knew he was coming to town, and the airport itself had been instructed to have all of their security working today.

For a few minutes of this guy walking through and out the door, Red thought.

As soon as they all entered the limo, Red drove away. He'd even been forced to drive them around, at least to the riverside area so they could get their photoshoots and smiles in.

Hed'd hoped this wasn't going to be a long, drawn out affair. Red had nothing special to do tonight but he'd rather be doing anything but this.

Red wasn't even all that political. He loved covering the news and liked being the first to uncover something important. The best part of this job was scooping another, more experienced reporter.

He chuckled to himself. He wasn't a reporter. Not really. A gopher who became a glorified gopher. He was a chauffeur today. Tomorrow he might be the chauffeur who dropped this idiot politician off at the airport.

The window between the front and the back was closed, and Red kept it that way. He didn't care about whatever they were talking about. He turned on the radio, very low, and groaned when a song was ending and the start of a thousand commercials was about to start.

I can't catch a break, Red thought. He turned off the radio and hoped the traffic wasn't going to be bad. He had a police escort but that didn't always stop cars ahead of them on I-295 from piling up.

Red wondered if they'd have food and drink at the ceremony. He was hungry and his stomach was growling.

The governor laughed loudly in the back, echoing through the glass.

Red knew this was going to be a very long day.

CHAPTER THREE

Karen Venzi was a jerk. Plain and simple. As soon as Red parked the limo she was at the door, helping the governor out, all while peppering him with questions that had nothing to do with today.

She worked for the rival channel's news, and she loved getting in Red's way. At first he thought she was flirting with him because she was interested, but then Red heard from the other reporters in the newsroom what Karen was really like: she was only interested in the story, only interested in throwing you off of your game, and only interested in women.

Red smiled when security pushed her away and kept knocking their shoulders against her microphone. No one liked her. It was rumored even her own bosses couldn't stand her, but she was aggressive and somehow, someway, got the scoop most of the time.

He made sure to ignore her as he walked with the governor and his team.

Karen walked off to likely get a front row seat and a great camera position.

About fifty feet from the podium, security stopped Red.

"Hey, no, I'm the driver and I'm with Channel 4 news and…"

Red was ignored, held back with a lot of other people. He could see there were checkpoints and only a few were being allowed to get to the rows of seats on the grass.

He swore under his breath when he saw Karen in the front row. She caught his eye with a smirk and waved. He wanted to give her the finger but knew with his luck he'd be photographed doing it.

Instead, he moved to his left as far as he could and got as far up as possible, which meant he was standing behind the rows of chairs with every other nobody. Not that he was actually doing more than driving the limo today, anyway.

Why am I even here? I don't care about any of this, Red thought.

If there was a way he could leave, he would, but he had to eventually drive these people around. He hoped it was back to the airport.

The governor was slowly making his way down the main aisle, shaking hands and kissing babies as he went, like all politicians do.

Red had such anger toward the man, but he didn't know why. Maybe politicians in general rubbed him the wrong way. You can always tell when a politician is lying because their lips are moving.

Ugh. I sound like my father, Red thought. He'd grown up in a very political household, his father a staunch Democrat and mother a tried and true Republican. They bickered about everything that had to do with politics, but nothing else. As long as the news wasn't on TV they were fine. He remembered all the nights of them sitting next to one another on the couch, sharing a bowl of popcorn, watching *Jeopardy*.

And then turning on the news and arguing for hours before one of them threw up their hands and went to bed first.

"Find a woman who pushes you, points out your faults and shows their own, can hold an argument with you for hours, and makes you see the world in her head and not only yours," his father had told him many times.

Red wanted a significant other that didn't want to talk or argue about politics. Ideally, she wouldn't agree with everything and she'd call him on his garbage, but not every night. Not try to hold his feet to the fire with anything he had an opinion on.

He wondered why he was thinking of his parents right now. They had nothing to do with anything he was currently doing.

The crowd was cheering as the governor stood at the podium, waving, the breeze in his thick hair as if he'd slipped Mother Nature a twenty to make him look good.

Besides the phone cameras clicking, the large news cameras were filming every angle of the governor, and he made sure to turn to get everyone involved.

Red's phone vibrated in his pocket. It was his boss, Bill Easdale.

"Mister Easdale, how are you today?" Red smiled. He loved being formal to Bill Easdale, since the man was very old school. He reminded Red of that Spider-Man newspaper guy, who hated the web-slinging hero.

"Did you manage to get the governor to the riverfront?"

Red sighed. "Yes. Aren't you watching the live coverage?"

"Not my job. My job is to make sure everything behind the scenes goes as planned," Easdale said. "Did it go as planned?"

"Yes, sir. He is standing at the podium as we speak, waving like an idiot."

"Yeah, well, that idiot will someday be our President and give us some big future ratings for live coverage, so drop your own feelings," Easdale said. "Make sure you drive the governor wherever he wants to go afterward. Got it?"

Red wanted to groan. He wanted to be done with all of this. "Of course, sir. Whatever the governor wants." *Hookers, crack, a good seafood combo. Anything.*

"Keep track of your time, too. I don't want you going over. Got it?"

"Yes, sir." Red wondered how he was going to manage his hours if the governor wanted to stay in Jacksonville for a few extra hours and get into trouble. The man had a reputation, to those like Red who knew a few things, that he had eclectic tastes. Illegal ones as well.

Rumor had it the last time he was in town he'd visited a massage parlor and gotten bad treatment, meaning he couldn't get it up and he complained. A week later the business was raided and everyone arrested. Very convenient.

While the governor was at the podium, a smile on his face and hands raised to the heavens, being so darn positive, Red wandered back and forth in the space allotted to nobodies like him. Even though he'd been the one to bring the governor to this spot.

"This area will be the most prominent spot in Jacksonville," the governor said loudly, the microphone feeding back. "Heck, maybe even in this great state of Florida."

The governor smiled even bigger, hands still raised, basking in the adulation from the frenzied crowd. He pointed at the camera crews hovering around him, and motioned with his hand for them to follow.

This seemed weird to Red, and definitely off-script.

The governor walked to the edge of the river, talking to the cameras as he moved. He was too far for anyone to hear what he was saying since he'd left the mics and the safety of the podium behind.

His security crew were hustling, keeping everyone back that tried to follow and trying to stay pace with him.

"This is a great time for Jacksonville," the governor screamed with glee.

His heels were on the cement wall, the water lapping up and nearly wetting his expensive shoes.

The governor raised his hands to the sky and the crowd cheered, as if he'd said something miraculous.

Red knew this guy wasn't going to be around for long, since he would be pushing for the Presidency soon enough, turning his back on all of these promises he'd made to Florida. He'd do the bare minimum, just enough to stay on the state's good side, to get their vote, and march off to D.C. and the next rung on the ladder.

He wasn't around long at all, as something very big, very wet and very pink rose from the river right behind the governor.

It had a small head, like one of those cheesy dinosaur CGIs you saw in the movies. Two big black eyes.

A row full of teeth it used to clamp down on the governor's head and drag him into the river.

The clapping stopped and everyone was silent for maybe four seconds, before the screaming and the panic set in.

CHAPTER FOUR

How Red ended up across the street with Karen Venzi was difficult to fathom. He thought for sure she'd take off her heels and dive into the St. Johns River to get the exclusive interview with the monster.

Instead, she'd been right behind Red.

"Did you see it? What… What was that? Did you…" Karen was shaking. Red moved to wrap his arms around her but stopped. He detested her so much.

Red started to walk back toward the riverfront, now that everyone had scattered to what they hoped was a safe distance. He wasn't going to stare over the wall into the river, but he wanted to get away from Karen and try to figure out what had actually happened.

No way a monster just snatched the governor of Florida into the water, after biting his head off, Red thought.

He didn't believe in monsters. Bigfoot was a myth. There was no way this thing, whatever it was, would kill a man in broad daylight, in front of hundreds of witnesses, in front of a live audience watching at home.

Could it be a hoax? Maybe the governor needed something to boost his ratings and somehow his people thought this would work. He'd eventually swim ashore, with his perfect smile, dragging the dead monster behind him. Triumphant.

He'd be the President that slayed a beast. *Time* covers. Him with a foot on the neck of the pink creature. Interview after interview, his story becoming bigger and bigger.

It reminded Red of the Seinfeld episode with the golf ball, when George rescued the whale.

The sea was angry that day… Easy big fella…

"Wait. Come back," Karen said.

A dozen police officers were forming a blockade, trying to get everyone away from the area, holding the smaller crowd back.

Red stopped a few feet away, trying to see past the cops. Looking for another breach of the monster, the head to pop back up, or part of the body to break the surface. A ripple in the water. Anything.

How long has that thing been here? Did it come in from the ocean, or has it been living in the St. Johns River for a long time? I need to know, Red thought.

He tried to think of someone with a big boat he could borrow. Go out with the person, at least. Try to find it. Record it. Get the scoop before someone like Karen got her wits back and pursued it.

Red finally gave up when the helicopters and more police arrived, escorting everyone up past Laura Street to the main library, where they wanted to interview witnesses.

Karen hooked his arm as they walked. She was no longer scared. She looked absolutely excited, talking a mile a minute. "What do you think it was? Are there more of them? Is the governor dead? Who gets the position now? What about the reason he was here, right? Will they close the park? Drain the river?"

Red sighed and kept walking. She had a death grip on him. If he was being honest, he liked the smell and feel of her so close to him, even though he couldn't stand her.

"Can you let go of me?" Red finally managed to get out of her grip and tried to walk back to the limo. Then what? There was no governor to drive back to the airport. The streets would soon be flooded with more news vans, more cameras and lights, and hundreds, if not thousands, of curious locals.

All trying to get the story, all trying to see where the monster killed the governor.

Red had no doubt the man was dead. Even from his distant spot on the grass, he thought he saw blood where his head had been. Before the creature grabbed him.

He walked up to the main library, figuring it was as good a spot as any. He didn't want to stay in the park and get jostled in the mob that was forming.

Karen found him, standing next to him with tears in her eyes. Babbling about how awful this was, how chaotic the scene had become down at the river.

Red did his best to ignore her, turning his back and pulling out his phone. He searched and quickly found live coverage.

A news chopper was low over the St. Johns River, moving slowly and the camera aimed at the surface of the water below. A news reporter off-camera was spitting gibberish about the *supposed* attack, saying nothing was verified at this point.

Red knew darn well it was verified because he'd seen it with his own eyes.

"There. Is that something?" Karen had slipped in next to him and was pointing at his camera, blocking his view.

Red couldn't see anything other than maybe the shadow of the chopper on the surface of the water. "I don't see anything…"

Karen tapped a manicured finger on the phone. "There. See it?"

"That could be anything," Red said, but he wasn't convinced it was a shadow now. It moved away from the chopper at a high rate of speed before fading away, as if whatever it was had gone further underwater.

Red wanted to get out on the water more than ever, to see if he could spot it again. Without getting attacked, of course.

Two fire trucks came down Laura Street, adding to the confusion. Red could see dozens of JSO officers trying to keep the crowds back and failing. Too many streets led right to the park, and unless you could block them all off there was no way to properly control the crowds.

It reminded Red of going to a Jaguars football game. The stadium was nearby, and parking was atrocious downtown. If you didn't get to the game four or five hours early to tailgate you had to park a mile away and walk it.

Red wasn't big into sports but he'd gone to a couple of football games over the years, mostly because he had free tickets and was trying to impress some girl. The same with going to a baseball game and seeing the local Jacksonville Jumbo Shrimp team. He wasn't interested in what was happening on the field, but the food was good and the crowd was fun.

Karen was yanking on his arm. "Come with me. I think we can get up onto the bridge and see better."

"Bridge? Nah. I have to wait by the limo," Red said. He didn't want to get a better view. He wanted to get a boat and get out on the water. "You go if you want."

Karen seemed to be thinking about it before she shook her head. "Nah. I'll stay with you."

"Why?"

She smiled. "I have a really good sixth sense. It's telling me you have a plan and you want me to go away so you can unspool it. Am I right?"

"No," Red lied.

Karen didn't seem convinced, staying as close to Red as possible with all of the people coming and going.

When her camera crew caught up with Karen, telling her they'd gotten the call for her to do an on-site report, she sighed and looked at Red. "Stay here. Gotta work, but I want to talk to you. I'm in with your plan."

As soon as she rushed away, microphone in hand, back toward the riverfront, Red took off back to the limo.

He could only wait for a phone call from his boss or what remained of the people he'd picked up at the airport to return to the limo.

Red had no clue what to do after that, though. He wanted to go home and forget about this for a bit, but knew he had to do something.

He called his oldest and most trusted friend, Mick. "Any chance you got a boat we can borrow from someone?"

CHAPTER FIVE

Mick shook his head, staring at the dark water of the river. "Are you sure this is safe, bruh?"

Red thought it'd be safer if Mick wasn't so drunk right now. He could barely stand, and Lord knows what else he had in his system.

The pair had been friends since first grade, when older kids were picking on him on the playground after school. Mick had swooped in out of nowhere, using his Superman backpack to slam one kid's face with such force he broke his nose, and then swung it around and knocked the other boy to the ground. Mick began stomping on both of the boys until Red pulled him off and thanked him.

Later, once they started hanging around together, he'd understand where all of Mick's aggression had come from: his parents were divorced and his father, back in those days, had been an up and coming professional wrestler. He'd been a star in a few territories, notably Florida, Texas and Georgia.

His father was always nice to Red, the few times he'd met him. A huge man, he had a huge laugh and was always wrestling around with Mick.

By the time they got to high school, his father was no longer around. Mick always said he'd moved to the Pacific Northwest and was the Oregon champion, but years later Red had looked it up.

Mick's dad had overdosed in a sleazy motel outside of Birmingham, where he'd just been fired from a wrestling organization for being too high to get into the ring that night.

They never talked about it and his dad was never brought up again.

In high school Mick was out of control. He'd dropped the wrestling team, even though he could've been a state champion. Started to drink and experiment with drugs. Red was no saint, but he wasn't half as bad as his childhood friend.

Mick had seemed to have gotten it together since high school, but Red worried he was a bottle away from killing himself.

"I don't wanna get eaten tonight," Mick said to Red and smiled. Even with only the dock light down the way, Red could see Mick's glassy eyes.

"Maybe we should do this tomorrow night," Red said. He shook his head. "Mick, I asked you not to drink tonight. This was going to be serious and dangerous and…"

Mick waved his hands. "I got this. Am I drunk? Nah. Do I feel really good right now? I sure do. Besides, I got the day off from the papermill tomorrow so I can sleep in once we're finished." He pointed at the three fishing poles at the bow of the boat. "And if we catch this monster we'll have seafood for a month, right?"

Red didn't share in the laughter as Mick got into the boat and went to start the engine.

"I can't do this, and you definitely can't," Red said. "Come on. We'll go to Denny's and I'll buy you pancakes."

Mick turned and pointed at Red, a serious look on his face. "I'll take you up on that offer… Once we have the monster in the boat."

Red shook his head. "Can't you get a bigger boat?"

Mick laughed again. "Funny. That's from *Jaws*, right?"

"No. That's a legit question." Red put his hand out. "Come on. We'll do this another night. There are probably a hundred boats out there, right now, looking for it. Best if we stay out of the way." He worried the Coast Guard or law enforcement was going to be on the water tonight and Mick would definitely get arrested for being drunk and piloting a boat.

Red couldn't see any lights out there, but they were miles away from the main parts of the St. Johns River. He worried Mick would ground them out here in the swamps before even getting to the river.

Being stuck in the mud with hundreds of gators around every bend was not on his bucket list, either.

Red started to walk back up the dock. "Hey, Mick, we'll meet again tomorrow. Maybe go out around lunchtime. I'll buy us sandwiches and some drinks." He didn't intend on buying anything with alcohol in it, hoping Mick might come sober in a few hours, or at least sobering up.

Mick was trying to start the engine but failing. His coordination was way off.

Red sighed and went back to the boat. "Hey, man, come on. Time to sleep this off. I knew this was a bad idea."

Mick sat down and chuckled. "Gimme a second to get my hands to do the right thing. I swear, this is gonna be epic. We're gonna catch us dinner for a week."

Red wasn't sure if the creature, whatever it was, would be edible. He figured it was even less edible with the governor in its stomach, too.

"Come on out of the boat," Red said.

Mick at first shook his head but he was slumping forward in the seat and waving his hand in the air.

"I'll be right with you," Mick said. "I just need to rest my eyes for a bit."

Red slumped against a pylon and waited a few minutes.

Mick began to snore, sitting up with his chin on his chest.

I can't leave him here. The bugs will eat him alive, Red thought.

"Come on, Mick. Time to go home." Red climbed onto the boat as gingerly as he could, but it started to rock. He fell to his knees and tried to balance his weight.

Mick kept on snoring.

Red shook Mick's leg, the nearest part of the guy to him. Now he was yelling to wake Mick up.

"What? I'm up. Stop screaming, bruh," Mick said and laughed. He looked around, smiling. "Did we catch it?"

"Yes. You reeled it in and I cut it up into nice chunks." Red stood slowly and stepped back onto the dock. He held out his hand and Mick actually took it.

"Nice. We'll cook them up on the grill tonight. I think I have some carrots in the freezer, too." Mick stepped onto the dock but he wobbled when he did it.

Red knew if Mick tipped back he wasn't going to be able to catch him or stop the fall. Mick was too big a guy, like his father had been.

"I'm fine, dude," Mick finally said, taking in a big breath of salty air. "Just need to clear my head a bit. Maybe sit down, too." He walked slowly to one of the dock boxes and sat down on it.

Red waited patiently for his friend to get his head cleared enough to leave.

"I'll give you a ride home. Leave your pickup here tonight," Red said.

Mick stared at Red. "You're a good friend. You know that?"

"I'd like to think so. Come on." Red held out his hand and Mick took it.

"What about my car?" Mick asked.

"I'll pick you up early, before I have to go to work. Drop you off. Deal?"

Mick nodded and grinned. "Tomorrow night we're gonna go fishing."

CHAPTER SIX

Bill Easdale was waiting for Red at the door. "Come into my office. Ignore all of these other idiots. Got it?"

Red did as he was told, walking through a gauntlet of reporters and office staff eager to hear what Red had witnessed, but Easdale was yelling so loudly for everyone to get some damn work done, he wasn't paying them to stand around and gossip.

"Sit," Easdale said when Red entered the office.

Easdale closed his door and yanked down the blinds before sitting behind his overly large desk, showing everyone he was the boss.

"Did you see the sub?" Easdale asked.

Red frowned. "What sub?"

"Initial reports were about a giant sea creature, but now we know it was a Russian submarine," Easdale said. "Did you happen to get any pictures with your phone?"

It took a second to realize his boss wasn't playing around with him. He was dead serious.

"There was no Russian sub. How would a sub go undetected all the way from the Atlantic Ocean into the St. Johns River, and then somehow rise up out of the water and bite down on the governor's head? That makes no sense," Red said. "Besides, there were cameras filming and broadcasting live to the news. Surely someone saw what it really was."

Easdale sat back in his chair. "And what was it, huh?"

"The St. Johns River Monster. I'm sure of it." Red sighed. He knew Easdale was going to start yelling, as always.

Instead, Easdale looked deflated. "Yeah… I know what you really saw. I know what a lot of people saw."

"Then what? I have a few ideas about this story. First, I can go through the archives. I remember my parents telling me about the monster. I even think years ago, when it was spotted by some fishermen, one of them was a distant relative to me," Red said, getting excited. He could do some interviews with whoever was left from back then. Maybe write a few different pieces for the newspaper.

"No. This is all being shut down," Easdale said. "What–"

Easdale had his hand up and he looked pissed as usual. "The government is pulling the plug on all of it. Every newspaper, every news channel. They're doctoring the photos. Changing the narrative."

Red slumped in his chair. "Why would they do that?"

Easdale looked ready to explode, hands shaking as he reached for his coffee cup. He picked it up and tipped it to drink and slammed it back on his desk. Red saw it was empty.

"Don't say a word," Easdale held his finger up to Red and then tapped it on his phone. "Jane, why is my coffee cup empty? Do you not like working for me, dear? Is this your way of trying to get fired and see if you can collect unemployment? Huh?"

Easdale had his finger back up and Red kept quiet.

A minute later, Jane, his secretary, rushed into the room with a steaming cup of coffee. She put it down on the desk, took the empty cup, and rushed back out.

"Now, what I think and what you know could get us in real trouble," Easdale said. He sipped his coffee.

Red needed a cup of coffee, too, but his boss hadn't even offered one. Like the jerk that he was.

"Then what do we do?" Red asked.

"Walk away. Forget it ever happened. Let the government do what needs to be done, right? They have a dead, missing governor on their plate right now," Easdale said. "I'm expecting the FBI, the CIA, ATF, Secret Service, Navy SEALs… every last person available to them to wash up on our riverbank and try to solve this."

Red shook his head but couldn't say anything.

Easdale put his hands up. "Look, I know you're disappointed. So am I. If I hadn't gotten this ultimatum, not only from the government but from my bosses, I'd shake it off and do some journalism things."

Red started to stand. "I guess we're done here, then?" He was so annoyed right now, because he knew what he'd seen. He knew what was out there.

"Sit down and shut up," Easdale screamed. He smiled and looked past Red. "That should get them listening."

Red sat down, confused.

Easdale leaned forward. "Here's the deal. I'm only saying it once. I don't chew my cabbage twice. Understand?"

Red did not understand but he nodded his head.

"I'm going to scream at you for another few minutes. Let these office monkeys think you're in real trouble. I'm also going to say you were suspended. I'll give you your pay, of course, but stay out of the office." Easdale handed Red a business card. "Here is my home number. Only call this. These lines might be tapped."

Red doubted the phone lines were tapped, but he nodded again.

"You need to leave here in a couple of minutes and drive to the airport to pick up someone," Easdale said.

Red groaned. Not another politician. Why was he being supposedly suspended if he was still going to pick up idiots from the airport, too?

"A guy I used to work with in Cleveland turned me on to this crazy, nutbag dude from Upstate New York. He has a cryptid program. Bigfoot and garbage like that. He goes out hunting for monsters, and from what my buddy told me, he's found a few," Easdale said.

Red didn't believe that for a second. He nodded again.

"Anyway, go pick him up and set him up in a hotel somewhere close to the airport. I talked to him early this morning and he's already on a plane. I also told him he had anything he needed, like a cameraman from our group." Easdale sighed. "The only guy I can vaguely trust is Derek Leeds. You know him?"

Red groaned. "No way am I working with him. He's such a jerk. There's a reason he's been fired from every other news outlet in Jacksonville."

Easdale waved his hand dismissively. "He's the only one I can trust, so make the most of it."

"Fine," Red said quietly. This was getting worse and worse.

"Use your credit card to get this guy a room and food. Whatever he needs. Once your suspension is over I'll reimburse you for whatever you spend. Deal?"

Red thought it was an awful deal, but what could he do? He needed to keep his job, and he'd be undercover, so to speak, while this person found the St. Johns River Monster. They'd be famous.

Or dead.

"Who is this guy, anyway? What's his name?" Red asked.

Easdale smiled. "Hunter Shaya."

CHAPTER SEVEN

Mick stared out at the gorgeous river and smiled. He was still hungover but a boat ride usually cleared his head. He was one with nature, he had no worries, and he also had a cooler at his feet.

Hair of the dog. A few cold ones and he'd be as good as new. Maybe even better. Red didn't understand Mick at all. If he did, he would've gone out with him last night and found this giant fish.

They'd be feasting on it right now. Mick thought having it over grits would be nice.

He opened up a beer, loving the pop as it called out for his lips.

Mick had everything he'd need. He hoped. Once Red dropped him back off at his pickup truck and said they'd go out tonight, Mick had agreed.

He was really going to go home and sleep a few more hours, but then he saw how nice the water looked. Calm. Peaceful.

The bug-out bag he always carried behind his seat came in handy. He lugged that to the boat and dropped it on the floor. Knew he had important things in there, like a box of crackers, spray cheese in a can, his .22, his Glock, lots of ammo, a couple of Braves ball caps, sunscreen and a small bottle of cheap bourbon.

Mick had his fishing poles and tackle box already on the boat. He'd need some big bait but thought what he had would do. He'd been shark fishing a few months ago and figured what he had left from that should work.

If he'd been thinking ahead of time, he would have driven off and gone straight to the bait shop. Gotten himself some bait for a monster, not that he had any idea what that would be.

Mick started the boat and took off from the dock, aiming for the middle of the river. This early there weren't too many other boats out. The ones that were out stayed closer to shore, which might keep them safe from the creature lurking in the depths.

Was there really something out here? Mick thought so. He might've seen it years ago, as a kid, when he was out with an uncle. The guy wasn't really his uncle, Mick thought, but some guy trying to make nice with Mick so he could have sex with his mom.

A distant hump on the water's surface had caught Mick's attention, but when he'd pointed it out the uncle had laughed, not even bothering to look, and said Mick had found the Loch Ness

Monster. It had made Mick upset and he'd cried when he'd gotten home.

If he remembered correctly, his mother had stopped seeing that uncle right after. Mick liked to think it was because the man was mean to him, but knew it was more likely he was mean to his mom.

Mick felt like he was being watched, but that was likely his paranoia. He knew being on the water drunk was going to get him in trouble, but Mick was also too nervous when he was sober to be out here.

Something splashed behind him and he turned so quickly he nearly lost his footing and tumbled into the St. Johns River.

"Probably a fish," Mick said. They had a couple of different fish that jumped out of the water this time of year. The splash wasn't too loud, meaning it was small.

Definitely smaller than a monster.

Mick decided he'd put one line in the water and spend a few hours searching for the creature. If he started to get bored or ran out of beer, he'd drop a second in and see what happened.

The fun of fishing wasn't always hauling in dozens of fish an hour, it was enjoying your quiet time. Letting your thoughts wander in and out and up and down.

Mick needed to clear his head every now and then. It reset his psyche, creating balance in chaos. At least, that's what the last therapist had told him.

The therapist had talked about his happy place, and Mick knew it was on a boat, alone or with a couple of buddies who knew enough to keep quiet unless needed.

Fishing and bringing in actual fish wasn't the first goal. It might not even be a goal at this point. Mick needed one fish pulled from the St. Johns River in order to eat every night. Some days he pulled a week's worth and spent the rest of the week happy to be on the water.

He wasn't going to tell Red he was out here today. Unless he caught the monster, of course.

Red was too high-strung at times, and Mick knew he'd be wound tightly until the monster was caught. Not that Red thought he was going to get eaten, but it was a news item he so desperately wanted to get the scoop on.

Mick laughed. His best friend was so different from him. A great guy and a great, loyal friend… but also a pain in the butt at times, because he never did anything even remotely wrong. Nothing even borderline illegal. He was on the straight and narrow path to goodness, to enlightenment.

Sometimes I envy him, Mick thought. He'd never admit it to Red. He wanted to do the right thing, wanted to be the better person, but he felt it wasn't in his DNA. He was the son of a former wrestler who'd thrown it all away. Completely.

Mick was supposed to be the screwup. That's all they ever saw in him and all he ever showed them.

"Stop whining and drink another beer," Mick said to his shadow on the boat.

He popped open a cold one and watched the line in the water.

Mick wiped the sweat from his brow with his ball cap. He waved at a couple of other fishermen as they moved slowly past.

"Catch the monster yet?" an old-timer asked with a toothless grin as he passed Mick.

Mick laughed. "Not yet. If you grab it, lemme know. I'd like to taste it."

"Maybe it'll taste like chicken… or whale. Delicious." The old-timer waved and kept moving.

The chance Mick was in the right spot wasn't very high. He doubted the creature was still hanging out near where he'd bitten into the governor and dragged him under.

Nothing had ever been filmed in the water, even back when they had businesses in that spot and security cameras aimed at everything. Not once in all those years had anything ever been seen.

Mick took out his phone and looked for the video of the attack again, but none of the local news sites had it anymore. Lots of articles about it, but no more videos. He wondered what had happened to it.

Mick wasn't much of a conspiracy theorist, but he knew when the news was being twisted and remodeled into something the American people could take and accept.

There was another splash, this one bigger, but he smiled. The fish were jumping today. Maybe he'd pull in something he could grill up for dinner.

His stomach roiled, the thought of good food making his mouth salivate and his thoughts happy.

Maybe tonight he'd invite Red over and they could have some food and beers before they searched for the river monster.

CHAPTER EIGHT

Hunter Shaya didn't walk off of the plane as much as swagger. He shrugged at Red, like he'd done this a million times. "Grab my bags, kid. I imagine they call you Red." Hunter waved his hand around his own head, signifying Red had red hair.

As if that wasn't obvious.

"Mister Shaya–"

"Please, Red, call me Hunter. I'm going to call you Red."

"That's what everyone calls me, so I'm good with that… Hunter."

Hunter dropped his two small bags at Red's feet. "Is there a bar in this airport? There has to be, right?"

Red tried to remain calm. The man was cocky. Arrogant. "We don't have time for a drink. There's work to do."

"All worka and no playa makes you an enemy of Hunter Shaya." The man laughed at his lame joke. "Gimme an hour and then we can go. I have three more bags at the carousel thingy, too."

Red wanted to scream. "What do your bags look like?"

Hunter spun around as he walked toward where he thought the bar would be. "Oh, Red, you'll know."

Red watched him walk away. The man was alone, when Red was under the assumption he'd have a crew with him. He knew the man's reputation as a publicity hog. He also knew the man got results.

If you believed the fantastical stories the man either told in the press or on his cable cryptid show, the man had found and battled many monsters, including a shape-shifting beast at the North or South Pole, chupacabra in an airport… again, if you believed these things existed.

Of course, we flew him in because there's a fantastical beast in the St. Johns River, so there is that, Red thought.

He went to the luggage carousel and immediately knew which three pieces of luggage was Hunter Shaya's: the three large suitcases with his smiling face on both sides of them and his name on the top and bottom.

Red groaned as he pulled them off and set them aside, wondering how to proceed. He had five bags in total to carry to the parking garage.

He tried to wave at a couple of people who looked like they worked in the airport, but they either didn't notice or ignored him, not wanting to help.

Red didn't blame them. He saw a JSO officer walking toward him and waved at the man, who smiled as he approached. "Need help with all those bags?"

"Yes, sir."

The officer got on his radio and smiled again. "They'll run out a cart for you in a few minutes. You're welcome." He walked off.

Red waited at least fifteen minutes before an annoyed woman arrived with a cart, ordered Red to bring it back to her when he was done, pointing at a door near the luggage carousel, and moved on.

"Thank you," Red called out. The woman ignored him. He stacked the luggage and made his way to the car. Easdale had let Red rent a car for the week so Hunter didn't have to ride in his beat-up excuse for a vehicle.

He put the bags in the trunk and the backseat and went in search of Hunter Shaya, who he found seated at a table in the bar with four other guys.

"Red, meet the crew," Hunter said. He lifted his nearly empty glass of beer. "Want a beer? Next round on you."

"No. We need to check into the hotel and get started," Red said and shook his head. "You didn't say there were five of you."

"Did you ask?" Hunter finished his beer and waved at the bartender for another round.

"No, I just assumed–"

Hunter laughed loudly and everyone in the bar looked at them. "You know what happens when you assume, right? Grab a chair, Red. We're gonna be here another couple of rounds at least."

Red grabbed an empty chair from a nearby table. He knew they needed to leave. He knew this was not going to end well, sitting here watching these five men get drunk.

"Hey, I only found three bags at the luggage claim," Red said.

Hunter pointed to a pile of bags in the corner. "They carried on two each as well."

"Then they need to carry them to the car. Not that there's room for them," Red said. He figured he needed to get tough with these guys or else they'd walk all over him.

Hunter looked stunned at first, but then Red saw he was busting chops.

All five men began to laugh.

"I guess you need to rent a bigger car. Maybe a bus," one of the men said. He reached out a thick hand. "I'm Fuji. I run the shots." The man was maybe Hawaiian. Nig, like a sumo wrestler. Red knew not to get on the bad side of this guy.

Hunter stood. "How rude of me. Let me do the introductions. Everyone, this is our Jacksonville tour guide, Red."

Red nodded. What else could he do?

"This is Bikini," Hunter said, pointing at a smaller man with a surfer haircut. "He does something."

Bikini shrugged. "I do something."

"Should I ask why they call you Bikini?" Red wasn't sure he wanted to know backstories on this crew. Better to be ignorant.

Bikini grinned and shook his head.

"Taco is our sound guy. That is not racist, by the way, even though he is Mexican. He won't give us his real name and insists we call him Taco," Hunter said, slapping the guy named Taco on the back.

"Pleased to meet you," Taco said. He was short and wore a San Diego Padres baseball cap on his head crookedly.

"Nice to meet you, too. Not sure how the Jacksonville tacos will be compared to where you grew up," Red said, trying to make conversation. So far, Taco seemed to be the nicest one with a genuine smile.

Taco laughed. "Man, I grew up in San Diego. I actually dislike most Mexican food. I hope you have Taco Bell. You can't beat a bean burrito."

"We do," Red said.

The last guy had his head and eyes down, hands clasped on the table like he was praying.

"Last and certainly least, our cameraman, Lester." Hunter put a finger to his lips and grinned.

"Lester had a bad flight. He gets sick. Every single time."

Red thought Lester shouldn't be drinking beer if he didn't feel good, but when the man looked up and stared at Red, through Red, he wisely kept his mouth shut and gave a quick wave.

Hunter came around the table and put an arm around Red's shoulders. He stunk of alcohol.

"So, Red… instead of hanging around and watching us drink, how about you go find us a vehicle that will fit all of us, huh? It sounds like you didn't prepare too well."

"No one told me there would be five of you," Red said.

Hunter burped, the smell making Red's eyes water.

"Do you think I carry my own camera? My own lighting rig? Scripts and notes and whatnot? Come on, Red. Use your head." For emphasis Hunter tapped Red on the top of his head.

Red knew he was in trouble. He wondered how long it would take for this crew to find the St. Johns River Monster so he could go back to his normal, boring life.

CHAPTER NINE

Mick didn't answer his phone, which was odd to Red. He never went anywhere without it, and Red hated when he answered while he was in the bathroom.

He'd dropped the five men off at the hotel, close to the airport, and said he'd swing by and pick them up in a couple of hours. Luckily the hotel didn't have a bar, or he'd lose them to another couple of hours of drinking.

Easdale had approved of the trade-in of his rental for a mini-van, although Hunter and his buddies spent the short ride to the hotel calling Red a soccer mom.

He wanted Mick to show Hunter's crew around and maybe get out on the water tonight for some B-roll and perhaps an actual search for the monster.

Red needed some sleep, too. He thought about asking Easdale for his own room at the hotel so he could be close to them, but knew it would be a mistake in two ways: Easdale wouldn't want to spend the money, and Red was afraid he'd get sucked into their party and get in trouble at some point.

He was far from an altar boy, but he knew these men were tried and true heavy drinkers. There wasn't ever going to be a couple of drinks and quiet conversation. They'd pound every beer and bourbon bottle they could find, get loud and obnoxious, and party until they dropped. Like overgrown and too-old high school bros, or maybe frat boys who never figured out the party was nearly over.

Red wasn't sure who was paying for all of the alcohol, either. Easdale said he'd worked out incidentals and the hotel room beforehand. Red was supposed to take them to breakfast, lunch and dinner for as long as they were in town working.

He wondered how all five of them were going to stay in one hotel room all week.

"I wonder how much the bill is going to be for the damage they cause," Red said aloud. He was driving to Mick's place, hoping his friend was home and in decent shape. Mick had a tendency to drink all day, which meant from very early in the morning until very early the next morning. If he'd started drinking yesterday, right after Red had talked to him, Mick would be in no shape to captain a boat ride for the visitors.

Red's phone rang and he frowned. It was his boss.

"You were supposed to call me as soon as they arrived," Easdale said. "Bring them to my office after five so I can speak to them."

"I just dropped them off at the hotel. After they landed, they decided to have a drink or five. They aren't in great shape but my goal is to get them on the water tonight with their fancy equipment and see if we can find something," Red said.

"Who paid for the drinks?"

"No idea. I'm guessing they did." Red pulled into a Publix parking lot because he didn't know what his next move was going to be. Where Easdale was likely to send him.

"I'm guessing they are going to hold onto the receipt and try to put it in at the end of this and have me pay for it." Easdale groaned. "I need you to stay with them. Make sure they're not up to no good. We don't need trouble. There's already enough going around with this supposed creature on the loose."

Red knew Hunter and his crew weren't going to pay for their own anything on this trip. "I'll cover for their meals when possible, but they'll likely order a lot of room service."

"Not if you're there, hanging out with them."

It was Red's turn to groan. "You booked them one room with two queen beds, for five grown men. Where am I going to stay, in the closet? Besides, they're not very, uh, friendly. They are a team that has worked on their own for a long time. I watched a few of their episodes last night. They have a camaraderie, like frat brothers. Very loose and lots of inside jokes. One of them is named Bikini, although that can't be his real name."

"Get another room next to them if possible. I'll reimburse you when this is all done," Easdale said.

"I'll need to see if I have any room on my credit card. I'm at about the limit and I still need to pay for their meals," Red said. "Any chance I can get a cash advance for the food or the room, or both?"

"No chance. The goal is to keep them focused so we can get the scoop on the monster. Then we push them onto an airplane and win a few awards for our coverage," Easdale said.

Red knew this was going to be like herding cats. "I'm going to take them to dinner tonight and then have a boat lined up we can use. I got this."

"I hope so. That pain in my butt Karen Venzi is sniffing around places, trying to work up a story. We need to beat her to the punch. Do what needs to be done and keep these guys in line while doing it." Easdale hung up on his end before Red could protest. He knew there was no way he'd get them to focus. It seemed like Hunter was here to drink as much as possible on their dime and then get a story for his cable show.

Red decided to go home and pack a bag. He had no clue how long this was going to take. He tried calling Mick again but his friend didn't answer.

He packed quickly, making sure he had his toothbrush and deodorant. He grabbed a couple of paperback books from his nightstand, too.

Red wondered what Karen was up to. They'd briefly connected after the governor's attack, but he didn't know if that still was the case. By now she'd gotten it together and was chasing the story. No way she'd want to talk to him, and if she got wind Hunter Shaya was in town she'd try to use Red to get to him.

Better to stay focused on what little Red could control.

He raced back to the hotel and tried to book a room close to Hunter and his crew. He managed to get on the same floor just down the hallway. Red was sure the noise from their room would keep him and the other guests up all night.

After putting his bags in the room and turning the air conditioning on as high as it would go, Red went down the hall and knocked on the door to Hunter's room.

After a few seconds he knocked again, a bit harder, fearing they'd left the room and were wandering around Jacksonville getting into trouble.

The door opened a crack and a bleary-eyed Fuji opened it a crack. "Hey, Red. What's up?"

"What are you all doing?"

"Nap time, dude. I'd invite you in but there isn't any room. I'm sleeping in the tub. My neck is killing me." Fuji smiled. "We need to find this monster and fast, or you'll be paying for my chiropractor, too."

Red knew he was going to regret this next thing but he felt bad for the guy. "I have a room down the hall. Two queen beds. You're welcome to crash there if–"

Fuji closed the door, leaving Red confused in the hallway.

A few seconds later Fuji slipped out and closed the door quietly behind him. "Let's go." He had his bags in hand. "Don't tell the other guys, though, or they'll want to come down there, too. I need my damn sleep."

Red led Fuji down the hall.

CHAPTER TEN

Brenda didn't trust the woman. She'd seen her on television every night, and her perfect teeth and her condescending smile always bothered Brenda.

"Ma'am, I'd love to have a few words with you," Karen Venzi said, standing at Brenda's door in her red pressed suit with matching heels and lipstick, a cameraman on Brenda's walkway. In front of the nosy neighbors who were starting to look out their windows or step onto their porches.

Brenda groaned and opened the door wider. "Get in here and hurry. I don't wanna be the local gossip again."

Karen stepped inside and kept the smile on her face. "My, what a lovely home you have."

"It's a dump. I'm a month behind on the rent. Lost my job and I need to work until the day I die. Lord willing that comes sooner than later." Brenda sat down on a chair facing the television and picked up her lit cigarette. "I'm guessing you're here because of Pinkie."

"Pinkie?" Karen went to sit on the couch but stopped short, the alarm in her eyes obvious.

Brenda figured the woman's red outfit cost more than all of the furniture in the house combined. "I can get you a towel," Brenda said.

"No. I'm fine. Of course not. Don't trouble yourself. I've been sitting all day," Karen said, her fake smile back again. "Just a few questions and we'll let you be. I can see you're busy."

Brenda chuckled. "Yeah, you're disrupting me from solving all of the world's problems."

"You said Pinkie." Karen sat on the very edge of the couch cushion, one buttock touching it. "Who is that?"

"The St. Johns River Monster. Duh." Brenda took a drag from her cigarette. "I called him Pinkie afterward, in the press, but it was 1975. There wasn't much interest back then. No one believed us. They thought we were young, stupid and drunk. Guess what? We were all of those things."

The cameraman took a step closer to Brenda, who smiled and took another drag. "Make sure you film me on my good side."

Brenda laughed, knowing she was the only one who got the joke. She was old, and she looked even older. She'd lived a hard life. The day on the river had changed her for the worse. She didn't want to talk about any of this, but figured she had nothing to lose at this point.

"Hey… am I going to get paid for this exclusive interview?" Brenda asked.

The question looked like it threw the reporter off for a second.

"Uh… we can buy you dinner. Order something for you," Karen said. "I can have GrubHub deliver some burgers. How's that sound?"

Brenda pointed at Karen. "I want a shrimp pizza. Ever have one from Dolce's? It is delicious. And a bottle of Coke and their meatball sub is really good, too. No money, though?"

Karen shook her head. "We aren't legally allowed to pay you for an interview. I have some documents in the truck we'll need you to sign." She turned and waved her hand to the third person in her team, who was standing behind the cameraman. He rushed back outside, likely to get the documents for Brenda to sign.

"Am I getting my shrimp pizza?" Brenda asked. She couldn't remember the last time she'd had enough money to buy a pizza. Usually, she ate tuna sandwiches or soup for her meals.

"I'll even order you breadsticks if they have them," Karen said.

Her smile was annoying Brenda, who looked away, into the camera. "Look at that guy or look at you?"

"You look at me, dear."

"Brenda."

"Brenda. Fine. As soon as we get the paperwork… here we go," Karen said.

The third person came in and placed a pen and a thick stack of paper in front of Brenda.

Karen was back on her feet, pointing at the spots Brenda needed to initial and/or sign.

Brenda didn't know if this was a smart move or if some other news agency would pay her actual cash, but as long as she got her pizza she was fine.

"And a meatball sub," Brenda said when she was done signing.

"Of course. Let me get reset." Karen sat back on the edge of the couch. She held up three fingers and slowly took one away. When she had just a fist in the air she plastered on the fake smile and introduced herself to the camera.

Then she turned toward Brenda. "Brenda, welcome."

Brenda nodded. She didn't want to smile and show her missing tooth. She might be an old woman now but she still had her pride.

"With the recent happening around town with the governor supposedly being attacked by a huge river monster… you had your own encounter with it many years ago. Right?" Karen smiled for the camera.

"Yep. 1975. Me and some friends were fishing on the St. Johns River. I saw it first. They didn't believe me until we were attacked. I lost a good friend that day." Brenda waited for Karen to ask what her friend's name was or a good followup question about the attack.

Brenda had never really told too many people about it. Initially, they all did a couple of radio or news interviews, but it quickly died down. No other sightings and Wallace's body was never recovered. The whisperings were they were all drinking heavily and Wallace had either gotten drunk and fell overboard, or there'd been a drunken fight and he'd been killed and tossed over the side of the boat.

Karen moved on with her set questions, acting like she didn't even hear the answer. "Why do you think this creature has returned? Is it because it doesn't like the governor's politics, or maybe the lack of funds to properly clean the river, or the fact he was going to officially announce his run for the Presidency?" Karen winked at the camera with a grin.

Brenda thought she was an even bigger idiot than at first glance. "I think the monster lives out in the ocean and maybe swings back through every fifty years or so."

"How old is the monster?" Karen asked, not looking at her notes.

Brenda frowned. "How the F should I know?"

Karen matched the frown. "We don't use that base language, ma'am. Let's cut that and you can think of your proper answer."

Brenda shook her head. "I said what I said. I'm not saying another word until you order my pizza."

Karen stood. "I think we have enough for now. Have a nice day, Barbara."

"Brenda, you stupid fake talking head." She knew she wasn't going to get her pizza. "You people are awful. I hope the St. Johns River Monster doesn't wait another fifty years to come back, because you'll be long dead with all your fake boobs and fake lips and the toxins injected into your body. I'd love for Pinkie to eat you. Get out of my house. Don't use my footage."

Karen scooped up the paperwork and laughed. "I'm sure we can use at least a line or two."

Brenda noticed the cameraman was shooting the pictures of her family on the wall and into the bedroom.

"Get out," Brenda yelled.

"We got what we came for," Karen said to the men with her. "Time to go."

Brenda slammed the door as soon as they left. She groaned. Why had she agreed to do that?

She truly hoped, if Pinkie was going to kill again, he'd find Karen Venzi, and take his time chomping on all of her plastic surgery bits.

CHAPTER ELEVEN

Red woke Fuji from his nap. The man snored so loud it felt like the room vibrated. "Time to get to work."

As Fuji used the bathroom, Red went down the hall and pounded on the door until Hunter answered, hungover and bleary-eyed.

"Time to get to work," Red said.

Hunter looked confused. "Huh? We'll find your river monster when the time is right. You can't rush this." Before Red could respond, Hunter slammed the door and Red heard the lock engage.

Fuji was standing in the hallway and shrugged. "We need to get some breakfast. Going downstairs?"

Red gave a shrug back and joined Fuji as they went down to the lobby.

"I was under the impression you guys were in town to find the monster," Red said. There was no breakfast spread except for coffee.

"They got a McDonalds around here? I could go for a Big Breakfast," Fuji said.

"There's a Dunkin just up the road."

"Even better," Fuji said. "Look, Red… things happen at a pace that Hunter sets. Alright? We'll get a ton of film in and maybe even see this watery beast. Doubtful, but we'll have something that visually works."

Red frowned. "What does that mean, visually works?"

They walked to the mini-van and got inside. It felt like it was a thousand degrees in it, even this early in the morning. Welcome to Florida.

"We can't come all the way down here and not see a monster, can we? No. If nothing else, there will be footage of a big wake in the water. Shadows and something big we'll find on a fish finder or with our equipment. This will be all worth it." Fuji smiled.

"No. You're here to actually find the St. Johns River Monster," Red said. "That's why we have you here. Not to make things up for your ratings."

Fuji chuckled. "You work for a news program on television. I guess your bosses don't care about ratings and advertising and money? You sound delusional, Red."

"No, that's different. We're at least trying to present the truth."

Now Fuji was really laughing.

Red was glad they pulled into the Dunkin parking lot and they went inside.

"I guess we need to get the rest of the crew something as well," Red said, knowing if he didn't they'd be asking for it and he'd need to do another trip. Further wasting time.

He ordered one of those big boxes of coffee along with a dozen donuts for Hunter and his crew. Red got himself a large coffee, light and sweet, and a cinnamon bagel with cream cheese.

Fuji asked for the same as Red but also added a bacon, egg and cheese on a bagel and four glazed donuts.

They sat inside and ate and sipped their coffees.

"How long have you been doing this?" Red asked.

Fuji glanced at the ceiling. "Six or seven years. About. Started working for Discovery Channel as a cameraman and then worked my way to various other jobs. I liked running shots. Directing. Landed with Hunter not even a year after I got into the business. He was looking for someone who could hold his own and get things done."

Red's phone rang. He groaned and took the call outside.

It was Easdale. "Are you out on the water yet? There's been another sighting. In Jacksonville Beach, under the bridge somewhere."

"Does the St. Johns even flow through there?" Red asked, not sure off the top of his head. "It could be a false sighting. I'm surprised we haven't had dozens of them yet."

"Whatever the case, you need to get out there before Karen Venzi does. Rumor has it she talked to Brenda Smith, one of the people that first saw the monster in the mid-1970s. If that goes live on tonight's news it will put us further behind," Easdale said.

"I'm talking to their set-up guy now and we'll be rolling shortly."

"I need footage. Have you spoken to Derek Leeds? He said you haven't called him yet. He's been ready to go since yesterday afternoon." Easdale groaned. "Don't make me regret putting you on this news, Red. This might be too big for you to handle."

"I got it, boss. I'll call Derek right now and have him meet us at Jax Beach."

Red went back inside and grabbed what was left of his bagel and coffee. "Time to roll. Do me a favor and call Hunter. We have a solid lead but we need to move quickly, before someone else gets it."

While Fuji was calling Hunter, Red called Derek and gave him the location where they'd be heading soon. Red knew he wasn't going to be able to use any footage Hunter shot unless they paid him handsomely for it. Hunter seemed to be that guy.

Red was surprised when he pulled up to the hotel and saw Hunter and the rest of his team waiting with their equipment. Without a word they loaded the gear and jumped in, thanking Red for the coffee and donuts.

Hunter looked refreshed and so did the others. Like they'd had a good night's rest and were up and ready to work.

"Where are we heading, Red?" Hunter asked. He was sitting behind Red, Fuji still up front.

"There's a report of a sighting near a bridge about half an hour or so from here, so we're heading over," Red said.

Red was happy they all seemed to be on the same page. Finally. Now maybe they could get to the bottom of this.

"I have a friend who has a boat we can go out on tonight," Red said.

"There's no time to take a pleasure cruise, Red. We have a monster to catch." Hunter smiled and put a hand on Red's shoulder. "I'm playing with you, of course. A boat would be great. We can find some divers, too, Red. See if your boss has a lead on any before another news agency hires all of the good ones."

Red was going to call Easdale once they arrived at the bridge.

"What are we doing for lunch?" Fuji asked Red.

"Nothing until we at least get some actual work in," Red said. He smiled. "Maybe tacos?"

Hunter laughed. "I was dreaming about tacos last night. I hope there's a good place in Jacksonville."

"Actually, not too far from where we're going. A place called TacoLu's. You have to try their scallop taco. Amazing." Red was now looking forward to getting some work in and then getting some food.

He doubted the monster had strayed from the St. Johns River and into the Intracoastal Waterway. While they connected, it just seemed unlikely to Red.

Why? His gut feeling, which usually amounted to nothing.

If this monster was now there, he'd be closer to an unsuspecting population. To so many docks and boats and people.

This would be a nightmare.

CHAPTER TWELVE

They began setting up on the bridge, lugging their equipment from a nearby business.

"I know the owner. Did a story on them a year or so ago, when the office was burned," Red said. D&D Recovery was a fixture in Jax Beach. If you were late or missed a few car or boat payments, you could expect this crew to grab your vehicle.

Red met Derek and had him set up with his camera aimed at Hunter and his team as well as checking the water below the bridge every now and then, just in case he caught a shape in the water.

"Follow their lead," Red told Derek. "I don't want to miss a thing. I also want enough B-roll footage for the future, too. This story might have some legs on it."

"It already has legs," Derek said, giving Red a look. He shook his head and aimed the camera at Hunter.

"I don't see much down there, but get the shot anyway," Hunter said. He turned to Red. "I thought you had a witness?"

Red called Easdale and got the information from him.

When he called the number a man answered and sounded excited. "Yeah, I saw it. Big and black and a mouth filled with razor-sharp teeth."

"It was black?" Red asked. He'd seen a glimpse of the creature and it looked pink to him. Of course, if the man had seen it from on top of the bridge, it might look black because of the sunlight and the water refracting, and a bunch of other scientific explanations beyond Red.

"Yeah, really dark. So black you could see yourself," the man said.

Red frowned. "Where were you standing when you saw it?"

"On top of the McCormick Bridge."

Red doubted the man had seen his own reflection in the black skin of the monster, especially since what he'd seen was pinkish, and the bridge was at least sixty feet high at the topmost point.

"Thank you, sir. I'll be in touch if we have further questions," Red said.

"Aren't you going to meet with me in person and do a proper interview? I took a shower and put on my Sunday best," the man said.

"Right now we're at the bridge shooting some footage, but like I said, I'll be in touch."

"I can be there in ten minutes. See you soon," the man said and disconnected the call.

Red didn't want the man to show up and talk about what he thought he'd seen. It was obvious to Red the man was either delusional or wanted to have his fifteen minutes of fame.

"What did the guy say?" Hunter was smiling at Red. "He swears he saw it from this height, right? Could tell the color of the creature's eyes. Read the license plate number dangling from the monster's mouth, eh?" Hunter shook his head. "I've run into people like this all the time."

"He's on his way," Red said.

"Obviously. I'll have Bikini walk him off the bridge and do a fake interview with him. Maybe record it so we can laugh about it over drinks tonight. Who can say?"

Red knew this was going to be a long day and they'd get nothing done that was concrete and helped with the story.

They filmed for awhile and then took a break, Fuji asking Red to drive him so they could get some cold water. The sun was brutal on top of the bridge.

Red drove them a couple of miles to a gas station, where he had to use his credit card to buy them cold drinks and a couple of bags of chips. He made sure to put the receipt in his pocket so he could get reimbursed at a later date.

Fuji was quiet the trip there and back.

"What's wrong?" Red finally asked as he parked in the repo business parking lot.

"I'm just… all this travel, man, is killing me. I love Hunter and the paycheck and the guys, but someday I hope to settle down and find a nice, quiet place all my own, you know?" Fuji sighed. "I'm getting too old for all of this. One week we're in Alaska and the next in Cuba. Thousands of miles, crisscrossing the globe, all for what? A basic cable show that not too many people watch. I was hoping by now we'd get some notoriety and be picked up by a major network."

"Maybe this will put you on their radar," Red said.

Fuji shook his head. "We've found a lot of actual cryptids. Hunter has an uncanny knack for going to where they are. Chupacabra. Bigfoot. Various other creatures. We have special episodes. Interview other legit people who shared the experience. Guess what? No one seems to care. They act like we're like every other paranormal and cryptid show. Lots of fake experiences, some CGI thrown in for good measure. Nothing substantial."

Red didn't know what to say. They were silent for nearly a minute before Fuji opened the door and let in the stifling heat.

Back on top of the bridge, Red decided to be more positive. He smiled at Hunter and especially his crew, knowing they were doing what they loved. Trying to find the truth out there, wherever it was. Wherever it took them.

"I'm ready for tacos," Hunter said. He clapped his hands. "Time to eat."

"But… we just started." Red couldn't believe how quickly they were breaking the equipment down. "That guy will be here soon."

"Which is all the more reason to get going," Hunter said.

A man was coming up the bridge and Red pointed him out.

Hunter smiled at Bikini. "Go meet this guy with the hand-held and get his story."

While Bikini met the guy halfway down the bridge, Hunter and his team carried the equipment past the man to the mini-van.

Red nodded at the guy but ran ahead to unlock the vehicle. He couldn't wait to crank the air conditioning.

As soon as everything was packed, Bikini came running over. "I got it. Whatever he thinks he saw. No clue. Might be nothing or he might have actually seen it."

Red didn't know and right now didn't care. All he thought about was tacos from TacoLu's.

He drove them over and parked.

"Will the stuff be safe here?" Lester asked.

Red shrugged. "As good as anywhere, I guess."

Hunter chuckled. "Do you remember the time we went to Detroit? That was hectic and scary."

Fuji slapped Red on the back. "You shoulda been there. We'd unloaded the van and took two steps when a dozen gangbangers surrounded us, wanting our equipment."

"Wow. What did you do?" Red asked.

Fuji pointed to Hunter. "He asked them if they were there for the audition. Said we were shooting a movie, a Detroit version of *Boyz N The Hood*. Said we needed them to go to Tiger Stadium and tell the person at the ticket window to give them their scripts and money."

Bikini laughed. "Their eyes lit up when they heard the word money, asking what they needed to do."

"Act like tough guys. That's it. A thousand dollars a day and the shoot will go on for at least a week," Fuji said. "They practically ran to the stadium."

"What did you all do?" Red asked.

Hunter smiled. "We jumped in the van and drove out of Detroit. We went back weeks later with an armed guard and no one messed with us, but it cost us a lot of money."

Red laughed with them, but he was hungry. "We should go inside and eat."

Hunter looked at the front of TacoLu's. "This place got a bar?"

"It does," Red said and figured they were never going to leave and get back to work.

CHAPTER THIRTEEN

Two hours later, while everyone was ordering shots of bourbon and tequila like they were going out of style, Red got a phone call. He walked to the outside deck and took it.

"Do you know a guy named Mick?"

Red swallowed. "Yes, sir." Mick was dead. Mick had choked on his own vomit in a drunken stupor. Mick had fallen overboard, drunk, and drowned. Mick was gone.

"Can you come and pick him up? This is JSO. We're down here at the Dunns Creek boat launch area and he's beyond drunk, sleeping in the bed of his pickup truck. We can't wake him."

Red smiled. Mick was drunk but alive.

"I'll be there in half an hour or so," Red said. He rushed back inside, intent on telling Hunter and his crew it was time to leave.

They didn't look ready to leave, ordering another round of shots as he came back to the bar.

"Our boat captain needs to be picked up, so it's time to go," Red said.

Hunter shook his head. "You go and pick him up and bring him back here. This place is awesome. I'm about to order another scallop taco."

Red didn't want to argue. "Don't leave," he said and left.

He was hoping Fuji would offer to come with him, but Fuji was looking at the menu.

Red left, worried they'd run the bar tab up past his credit card limit.

"What did you get yourself into now, Mick?" Red asked as he drove. Of course, it was better than his friend having something bad happen to him. Knowing Mick, he hadn't gone straight home last night. He'd gotten drunk and gotten on the water.

If anything had happened to him, Red would've felt bad. Worse than bad. Mick was his best friend, his brother, his confidant.

The joke was always to find someone who'd help you bury the bodies. Mick would grind the bodies in a woodchipper if Red needed it done. He'd not only give you the shirt off of his back, but Mick would do his best to knit you a shirt if need be.

Red always worried he wasn't the perfect friend back to Mick. He spent a lot of time complaining about his life, trying to talk Mick into not drinking so much and looking for real, steady work. Was he being a good friend by getting on Mick's case all the time? Red didn't think so. He'd need to tone it down a bit.

"It's not like my life is so great," Red said. "I'm not going anywhere in my job or my life."

Red hadn't had a steady girlfriend in forever. He wasn't close to anyone but Mick. He spent his money on dumb things and barely scraped by with his rent and bills. He was getting too old to keep doing this, and he knew it.

As much as he wanted to be a live personality on the news, he knew Easdale was never going to let it happen. His boss thought he was good enough in the spot he was at, and there would never be a promotion or a raise.

Red was a step above the interns at the station. He was a gopher, picking people up at the airport and getting Easdale coffee when his secretary wasn't available.

He knew the cop that was standing with Mick, who was leaning on the back of his truck.

"I'm gonna hand him off to you before he does something stupid," the cop said to Red and nodded before getting in his police cruiser and leaving the parking lot.

Mick was smiling. He rubbed his bloodshot eyes. "I'm not gonna do anything stupid. I'm drunk. I'm not driving. I don't even know where my keys are."

Red found the keys on the front seat of the pickup truck. He asked Mick where his boat was.

Mick turned and pointed back to the dock. "I tied her up nice and proper. You know me, Red… no matter how drunk I get, I can still handle a boat better than anyone. I made sure to get the boat docked and my stuff out of it before I started the heavy drinking." Mick grinned. "Want a beer?"

"No. I want you to stop drinking today. I need you to take me and the film crew out tonight on the boat, but I can't do it unless you're sober," Red said.

"How about sober-ish? You know I'm good right now, and a couple of hours of coffee will get me closer. Or…" Mick was grinning again. "Hair of the dog. I can get to the perfect sweet spot of drinking, where I can still handle the boat without a hitch but no headache coming. Win-win, Red."

"No more drinking," Red said. "Come on. I need to pick up the crew at TacoLu's and then we need to come back and leave immediately."

Mick stopped grinning. "Sure, no problem… except one little problem."

Red wanted to groan but remembered his self-talk on the ride over, being a better friend to Mick. "What is it?"

"I have another passenger tonight," Mick said.

"No. I told you I wanted to hire you for tonight, to hunt the monster."

"Yeah, well so does this other person, and I could really use the money. They wanted to hire me exclusively but I told them there wasn't enough money in the world for me to do that to my best friend, so they'd have to come along with us." Mick smiled. "Money is good."

"I suppose it is," Red said. "Should I even ask who's coming with us?"

"Nah, it's a surprise. Plus, I'm not really sure who I talked to. It was while I was trying to sleep it off in the bed of the truck. I'm sure it will be fine," Mick said.

Red knew this was going to be anything but fine, especially since Hunter and his crew were going to be very drunk by the time they got onto the boat.

"TacoLu's, huh? A few tacos will sober me up," Mick said. "Also, a couple of shots will hit the spot, too."

"No. Absolutely not. I'll go in and you wait in the car." Red shook his head. He knew if Mick went inside with the other alcoholics he'd never get them on the boat.

"Fine. I want some tacos and I'll be good." Mick slumped down in the passenger seat and closed his eyes. Within a mile he was snoring loudly.

Red drove back to the restaurant and parked, leaving the sleeping Mick.

Hunter and his crew were still at the bar and they had a crowd. Red noticed the owner, Dan, was one of the people listening to stories from Hunter Shaya.

"And then the creature absorbed the guy into its gelatinous body," Hunter was saying. He spotted Red and held up a finger.

Everyone was silent. Hunter turned slowly toward two twenty-something girls seated near him. "The body was gone inside, you see? I looked closer. Maybe I could save the guy from the alien that had taken him." Hunter leaned forward a bit, as if he were staring into the alien.

Both girls were on the edge of their seats.

Hunter started to shake his head. "No, I didn't see him. No, wait…" Hunter raised his hands and screamed.

One of the girls fell off of her stool and the other screamed back. Red laughed because a lot of the audience screamed as well.

Hunter laughed and turned to his crew. "Time to go and hunt down the St. Johns Monster."

Red saw how everyone looked impressed at this mighty warrior showing up to slay the beast.

Hunter waved Red over and leaned in. "I am really, really drunk. I'm gonna lean on you out the door. Got it?"

"Sure," Red said, looking around. "Where's Derek and Fuji?"

"They went out on a beer run."

Red shook his head. "We're in a bar."

"We need beer for the boat ride."

Red knew this was going to be a problem, especially with Mick still drunk.

He'd need to drive through the nearest Dunkin and get a lot of coffee as well.

CHAPTER FOURTEEN

"How's everyone in the sunlight doing?" Grant asked Quinn when they met in one of the empty staterooms. The cruise ship was scheduled to leave JAXPORT within a few hours, and everything they had on their plates was ready to go. The passengers would be boarding soon.

"In an hour I'll wish I was down in the bowels of the ship with you instead of catering to idiots with their stupid requests," Quinn said. He hugged his boyfriend. "I'm looking forward to getting some sleep. These quick turnarounds are killing me. I'm not as young as I used to be."

Grant had been doing this work for two years but Quinn had been working on cruise ships for over twenty years. He ran the lido deck, taking care of the pools and the bars and the main buffet area.

Quinn also ran guests towels and explained to them about how the food and drinks worked, as well as answering questions about the various excursions off the ship in the next few days.

"I guess we'll both be hot and sweaty," Grant said, shaking his head. He knew he was starting at the bottom, literally, but he'd need to keep working hard and moving up the ladder to a decent job. The pay was great but it meant he was on the water for months and sometimes years, his home away from home.

They'd met when Grant had first started, a sly smile here and there during their dinners. They'd spent time together, feeling each other out, before Quinn, ten years older, finally asked Grant on a date.

Now a package deal, they'd worked all over the world. Not that they'd seen much of it, except from the upper decks of a cruise ship, but it was a good life.

They were going to get a quick bite with the rest of the crew when something struck the side of the boat.

"What was that?" Grant asked, nearly falling to the floor. The boat rocked but steadied itself a second later.

They went to the buffet area and saw everyone else was as confused as they were.

"This is the captain speaking. I need everyone to go to your quarters and stay there until further notice. Stay away from the sides of the boat and off of any balconies," was the announcement.

A few people moaned, wanting to eat before the guests arrived.

"Like any of us have balconies. Please," Grant said and a few people laughed.

They were herded to their rooms with lots of grumbling.

"If there's a problem with the ship, we should be evacuated, right?" Quinn asked.

"That does sound like the right plan, which means this is nothing."

Quinn shook his head. "The boat moved. We both felt it. We all felt it. We should abandon ship."

Grant stopped. "And what if we're wrong? What if it's something simple? We could be fired."

"Not a chance. Not this close to departing. We'll get called into an office and yelled at. We're not going to leave or go far, just get off the ship and see what's happening before we get back onboard. I bet no one will even know we're gone. Come on," Quinn said.

They took the next left turn and kept moving.

In a few minutes they were off the ship, acting like they were supposed to be leaving. No one questioned them. Quinn had taught Grant to act like you were on a mission, focused ahead of you and not smiling, so people got out of the way.

It worked. They were outside and moved away from the passengers, who were lined up to pile inside the cruise ship and spend the next few days ordering the staff around and acting like they were important.

The ship shuddered again and Grant and Quinn exchanged looks. What was happening?

"Maybe there's a problem with the waves or something. I dunno," Quinn said. He walked over to the side of the dock but the water looked calm, although there were ripples from the cruise ship shaking. The day was gorgeous, only a few clouds in the sky. Hazy and humid and typical Florida weather.

"Maybe one of the tugboats is going by too fast in the open channel?" Grant asked. "Not likely, though. That isn't going to make the ship move like that."

The cruise ship rocked again, inches from slamming into the bulkhead. There were security things in place like bumpers, but it was still unnerving to be down on the dock and seeing this massive ship towering above you, moving so erratically.

Quinn pointed up at the lido deck, where several of the crewmembers were looking over the side.

There was another shudder from the ship and it rocked violently, like it was a toy on a string and a child was yanking it around.

"They need to abandon the ship," Grant said, taking a step toward the crew on the dock with them.

Quinn grabbed his boyfriend's arm. "It's too dangerous. We can't go back inside."

"We can't do nothing," Grant shouted and pulled away from Quinn. He ran to the front of the line, inches from the two smiling women who were about to let the passengers board the ship.

"You need to call the captain before you open those velvet ropes. There's something wrong. If you let these people on the ship, they'll die," Grant said quietly.

"Aren't you supposed to be on the ship, waiting to take care of all of these paying customers?" One of the women, who Grant didn't know personally but had seen before, was giving him her big, fake smile. "You shouldn't be out here. Are you late? That's not very responsible."

Grant gave the woman the middle finger and turned toward the would-be passengers in line. He noticed Quinn off to the side, shaking his head.

"I am asking everyone to not get onto the ship at this time. There seems to be a problem and we need to figure out what that is before we can open the gate and let everyone inside," Grant said.

The woman was waving her hands over her head. "I'm going to need two lines, people. Straighten them out and have your documents ready."

Grant turned back to her. "Are you insane?"

"I am doing my job, unlike you," she said.

Grant stood in the way. "You can open the gate but I won't let anyone pass until you call your boss and ask what's happening on the ship. This isn't normal."

The woman turned to the other crewmember standing behind her. "This dude is so fired. Call and see what's happening. Tell them we have an idiot out here holding us up, too."

Quinn walked over and whispered in Grant's ear. "Time to move over. You said what needed to be said."

"If anyone dies and I let them walk into the boat and didn't stop them… I can't believe you, of all people, don't get that or get who I am." Grant was annoyed, at his boyfriend and this woman and all of it. He looked down the line at all of the people. All of the children.

They were all looking at him with anger in their eyes, as if he alone was the reason they couldn't board the cruise ship.

"I'm not moving," Grant said.

The woman's phone rang and she answered it, turning her back to Grant as she spoke quietly to whoever was on the line. When she turned back she shot Grant a dirty look. "We're going to board in a few minutes. There seems to be a slight technical difficulty but we will make up for the missed time when we sail, so there is no change in plans."

Grant stood his ground, hoping she wasn't trying to trick him into moving and then open the lines to board.

The ship made a grinding noise, and Grant turned to see the boat was tipping in their direction, a shadow over the first few rows of people.

The door to enter the ship exploded open, and crew members began pouring out.

"Move, you idiot," Grant yelled at the woman as she stood dumbfounded in the way. He grabbed her by the arm and pulled her away, yelling for the other woman to open the gate.

She was also paralyzed as more people came rushing from the boat. The gangplank was bending under the strain of the ship on such an angle, and Grant knew it wouldn't be long before it snapped and the only escape from the ship was by jumping into the water.

He began grabbing at people to help get past them and get to the gate to swing it open, before the small area was overflowing and crew members had to plunge into the water.

There was a noise like metal scraping metal, and Grant looked up in time to see some of the lifeboats hanging above them were dangling in the air.

Grant didn't have time to shout to run before one detached from its cable and fell on top of him.

CHAPTER FIFTEEN

Red's phone rang as he drove so he put it on speakerphone. It was Easdale.

"Hey, boss. You're on speakerphone. Everyone say hi to Mister Easdale," Red said.

Everyone in the mini-van started to scream and laugh and say hello.

"Are you at a party?" Easdale asked.

"No. We are leaving TacoLu's and heading out. Why? Got something solid for us?" Red hoped he did, because right now Red was going to drive around until everyone calmed down a bit. No sense in them still being wild and getting to the boat just yet.

"Head to the port. One of the cruise ships was attacked. Looks like the monster punched a hole in it at the waterline and it is sinking. People are dead or dying. Make sure Derek gets some good footage," Easdale said.

"Wow, boss, that is pretty cold, even for you." Red glanced at Mick, who looked better than he had when he'd first picked him up. "I'll head to the boat we've commissioned and head that way, so we have footage from the water."

"Excellent idea," Easdale said.

As soon as they hung up, Red called Derek and told him to meet them at Mick's boat.

"Looks like we got us a monster," Hunter said and laughed.

While the group talked excitedly in the back of the mini-van, Mick looked over at Red. "Bro, are you alright?"

Red chuckled. "Of course. Why?"

"You seem off. Worried about everything like you always do."

"No, I don't," Red said defensively.

Mick laughed. "Yes, you do. I worry about nothing. We are opposites, which is why we're so close. I figured you understood that a long time ago."

"I never thought about it," Red said. He glanced back at Hunter's crew, talking about setting up their equipment on the boat. "Listen… I need you to be very professional on the boat today."

Mick groaned. "What does that mean, bro?"

"You know what it means. Don't get sucked into their shenanigans. They're going to be drinking and carrying on and being ridiculous. I need our team, you and Derek and me, to do this the right way. This could make all of us, you know? You could be the captain who had a part in seeing or even hooking the St. Johns River Monster. That would look good on your resume."

Mick shook his head. "They'll still mostly talk about my dad, like any other time I'm mentioned in the newspaper or on the news."

Red laughed. "Maybe this time the article won't be about you being arrested for public intoxication."

"Stranger things have happened," Mick said. "I hear there's an opening in the governor's office. Maybe after I catch the monster I'll go into politics."

"Too soon," Red said.

"So… I guess I need to prepare you for our extra guest. Please don't flip out on me." Mick smiled. "We all need to act professionally, right?"

"Who is it?" Red asked, having an idea who it would be.

"Karen Venzi." Mick shrank away as if he was going to be punched.

Red wanted to punch Mick. "Please tell me you're joking. Please."

"She paid me way over my normal rate. She's coming alone, too, so only one extra passenger," Mick said.

"One extra too many. You know I don't like her," Red said. He shook his head. "This is such a backstab, bro."

Mick looked like he was going to cry. "No. This'll be good. Trust me. What's the expression? Keep your enemies close?"

"This is too close. I'd rather she had to find another way to get on the water. Maybe she won't show. Maybe she'll think we're not leaving until later." Red knew he couldn't really blame Mick. He needed the money, and Mick didn't fully comprehend how much Red despised the news reporter or the competition they were in.

"It'll be fun. You'll see." Mick smiled. "Besides, the way you talk about her all the time tells me you're sweet on her."

"Am not," Red said defensively, like he was six and was caught staring at a girl.

Mick laughed.

"What's the name of the place we're heading to again?" Hunter asked from the backseat.

"It's JAXPORT, where the cruise ships come and go. All the cargo comes in and out, too. There's a strip of land nearby, called Quarantine Island, where the first sighting occurred." Red had glanced at his phone and the ongoing messages from Easdale as the story developed, even though he was driving.

"Quarantine Island? That's excellent," Hunter said and clapped. "Make sure we get lots of B-roll of it. We might be able to use it in the future if we come back for something else."

"There's all kinds of monsters in this part of the state," Mick said.

"That means we'll be back someday," Hunter said.

Red locked eyes with Fuji in the back, who smiled and shook his head. Red knew Fuji wanted out at some point, maybe soon.

As much as Red loved and wanted so badly to be a reporter, he wondered if he could manage being on the road so much. Constant flights and long car rides. Seeing the world but only small parts of it at a time.

Like being a rockstar, Red thought.

He pulled into the parking lot again and parked next to Mick's truck.

"Nice ride," Karen said as she strolled up to Red and smiled. She glanced at the mini-van again with a grin. "Does your mom know you're driving her car? Who's gonna pick up your little brother from soccer practice?"

"Very funny," Red said, more annoyed than he should be. "One false move and I'll tell my friend, Captain Mick, to not let you on the boat."

"Doubtful he'd do it," Karen said and smiled at Mick, who blushed and looked away. "Let's get this show on the road. We have a monster to see."

Red wanted her to get back into her black SUV illegally parked on the curb and leave. This was going to be a nightmare having her along for the ride.

Maybe I can talk Hunter into not letting her go, Red thought. *After all, it is his charter. Technically.*

Red turned to see if Hunter could chat privately, but it was too late.

"Ahh, and who is this lovely lady?" Hunter asked, walking up to Karen and extending his hand. His smile was brighter than a hundred light bulbs.

Red knew he'd already lost the argument.

CHAPTER SIXTEEN

"This isn't right," Red said to Hunter, after Hunter helped Karen onto the boat.

"Relax, kid. This is going to be quite the adventure." Hunter was staring at Karen's butt as she moved. "A really nice adventure."

"Listen… she can't use your footage. We signed an exclusive deal–"

Hunter smiled and shook his head. "No, you did not. You signed a normal deal because your boss is cheap. I can sell this footage to whoever I want. He assumed no one else would be smart enough to step in, but…" Hunter smiled at Karen, who'd been listening. "I'll tell you what they paid me and then you can match it if you'd like. Considering you don't have a cameraman onboard…"

Karen nodded. "Deal."

"He didn't even tell you what we paid," Red said.

Karen shrugged. "My boss isn't cheap like Easdale. Give me the form and I'll sign it right now."

"We can do a digital signing," Hunter said and had his phone out.

"I need everyone to sit," Mick said. "If we want to arrive before all of the fun is over, I'll need to do some speeding."

Red stared at Mick.

"I got this. I drive much better with a buzz than stone cold sober, and you know it, Red." Mick watched as everyone sat down and made sure the equipment was in a good spot before he started the engine.

Red sat back and watched everything get away from him. Easdale was going to lose his mind when he found out about this. He wondered if he'd have a job, no matter what the outcome of tonight was. Unless they managed to capture the monster and Red got to hold it up on the dock, smiling, while everyone took his picture, he thought he'd be looking for other work soon enough.

He didn't blame Mick for taking Karen onboard to begin with. He didn't blame Hunter for taking the money for footage he was going to shoot, anyway.

It was his boss, Easdale, who was to blame. Because he was cheap and thought he was getting away with it, he'd purposely done the bare minimum.

Now it was biting Red, because he knew Karen would flirt and bully her way to get the best footage from Hunter's team. No matter what Derek filmed, Easdale would complain about it. The news shots

Karen got today would be infinitely better, and Easdale would ridicule Red and Derek about being incompetent. That was how he ran his newsroom. He put you down so you worried about your job and never asked for a raise or a promotion, because Easdale didn't think you were worth it.

After a while, you didn't think you were worth it, either.

Am I worth it anymore? Have I hit the wall with this job? I need to reevaluate my darn life, Red thought.

He couldn't stop staring at Karen, who'd settled in right next to Hunter and was laughing at one of his jokes.

Fuji looked at Red and shrugged. From the way he did it, Red thought maybe Fuji was under the impression Red had a thing for Karen. It couldn't be further from the truth.

Actually, I've always had a thing for her, and it has nothing to do with the business or work, Red thought, admitting to himself he was very attracted to Karen.

Even though she was scheming and underhanded and would toss Red off the side if given a chance.

Red shook his head and looked back the way they'd come. Mick was doing a fine job at keeping the boat on course and steady, but he was always a great captain. They'd spent many weekends out here fishing and cruising around and talking about their bright futures.

Now Red knew it had all been a waste of time. Neither of them were going to amount to much. Mick was going to drink himself to death, fighting the demons inside about his father, and Red was never going to feel satisfied in his work.

Not with Karen Venzi around, Red thought.

Karen was laughing at some lame joke Hunter had told her, and Red saw the rest of his crew were frowning and shaking their heads. They'd likely seen Hunter do this a thousand times, hitting on some local woman, who thought they were using him for a story. Red knew it was the other way around.

Red decided to stop feeling sorry for himself and do his darn job, whatever may come of it. He wasn't a quitter. He walked up to Derek and put a hand on his shoulder. "We need all the footage, bro. Got it? Film anything and everything. Don't worry about anyone else. This is our ticket to do something big. Are you with me?"

"You got it, boss," Derek said with a smile. "Have you talked to Easdale yet?"

Red shook his head. "I'm going to guess he'll be calling any second." He walked over to Mick and smiled. "How's it going?"

"It is going," Mick said. He was sweating profusely but holding the boat steady. They were going very fast but Red knew they needed to get to the action as soon as possible.

"You know I appreciate you, right?" Red asked Mick.

Mick tilted his head and frowned. "Are you dying or something?"

Red laughed. "No. I just… I never tell you that. I do love that we've been friends for so long. That you always have my back."

"Is this some setup because I let that hot news lady on the boat?"

"No, bro. I'm being real," Red said.

"I don't like when you're real. I'd rather we joked and had a beer," Mick said.

"Who needs a beer?" Hunter pointed at Mick and tossed him a cold one.

Red was about to argue they shouldn't be drinking on the boat, especially Mick, but he knew his words would be drowned out in the wind and the laughing.

Everyone except Red had a beer in hand now, and they were saluting the St. Johns River Monster and anything else they could give a toast about.

Red shook his head but didn't say a word. He needed to stay sharp. He was especially surprised to see Karen drinking a beer, but then he saw the faraway look in her eyes.

She was scared.

Red's phone rang. He turned away from everyone and answered it.

Easdale was beside himself when he found out Karen was on the boat, and she'd paid to use Hunter's footage, too.

"You never signed an exclusive deal with them," Red said quietly, trying to keep his back to Karen so she didn't hear his conversation.

"Tell that jerk Hunter Shaya we had a gentleman's agreement. This is unprofessional," Easdale said.

"Actually, what you did and are doing is the unprofessional part." Red decided to say what was on his mind and get ahead of his imminent firing. He'd speak his mind and see what Easdale did, while knowing Red was on the verge of getting the scoop. The big story.

So far there were no helicopters in the sky, so another news agency hadn't gotten wind of anything wrong yet. Red hoped this worked to his advantage.

"How dare you," Easdale said, obviously shocked Red was being so blatantly honest with him.

"I'm sick of you being so cheap, above and beyond what the station and your superiors give you," Red said. "Coming in each quarter well under budget isn't something to brag about. It means you have a very underpaid staff. It means you're a bully and you only care about the bottom line. Not the news. Not the people who bring you the news."

"I'd shut my mouth right now if I were you, Red, unless you want to start filling out unemployment forms."

Red glanced at Derek, who was staring at him.

I have a decision to make. Right here and right now, Red thought. I could shut my mouth and keep my job, or say what needs to be said and lose my job.

Derek gave him a subtle nod.

"You can take this job and shove it," Red said. "I quit. I'm not interested in working for such a jerk."

Easdale was livid. Red could feel it through the phone line. "Put Derek on the phone," Easdale said through obviously gritted teeth.

Red held out the phone to Derek, who shook his head.

"I'm with you. Where you go, I go, Red."

Red smiled. "Derek feels the same way as I do. We both quit. Taking a walk. Maybe Karen and her team will hire us for better pay, better hours and a chance for promotion."

Easdale disconnected the call.

Red laughed. He almost asked for a beer. He'd need to figure out how to turn in all these receipts and then find another job, but right now, at this moment, he was happier than he'd been in years.

CHAPTER SEVENTEEN

Red noticed the smoke first as they rounded the bend. He was all set to show Hunter Quarantine Island in the distance and give him a few facts. Maybe he could get a small segment or at least a shot of himself in Hunter's series. Might as well get as much out of this as he could, because he was out of a job.

I really don't need to do this anymore, Red thought. *I could have Mick drop me off at a nearby dock and I can go home.*

He knew this was getting exciting and being paid or not paid wasn't the interesting part right now.

Everyone crowded up front, and Red snapped his fingers at Derek to begin filming. This might be a good opening shot for a segment, which he could sell to another news agency. If Derek got anything really good it might mean going national.

"The cruise ship is on fire?" Karen asked.

"The boat is sinking," Hunter said with glee. He turned to Lester. "I hope to God you're getting this."

"Of course, boss," Lester said, camera on his shoulder. He was standing next to Derek, also filming.

Mick charged ahead, not slowing down as the cruise ship, or what was left of it, came into better focus.

The ship was nearly on its side, leaning against the dock. There were a couple of gaping holes in the side where it would usually be just above surface level.

At least three holes and at least twice as many fires. The engine room might have been exposed.

Red searched the water for any signs of the monster, but except for the ship and the screaming people on the dock, everything was serene. The water was calm. Peaceful.

Hunter was pointing toward the center of the river. "Is that it?"

Red leaned over the side to get a better look, but the sun was shining down in the spot Hunter was looking at, obscuring the view. It could be a school of fish, it could be a shadow of a passing cloud, it could be anything.

"Get closer to the boat or to where he's pointing?" Mick asked Red.

Red didn't know the answer. They might be chasing nothing more than a shadow, or actually get close to the monster.

The burning ship was an actual event they could film and use.

"The shadow. I see it, too," Karen yelled to Mick.

Mick headed in that direction. Red pointed at the cruise ship and told Derek to keep filming it until they definitely saw a monster in the water.

Red hoped it wasn't in the water because he didn't want Karen to be right. He wanted to gain some control over this day, knowing it wasn't going to happen.

He knew he was being petty and he might be screwing himself by not getting the shot from Derek and not being the first to see the monster, but Red was angry.

Angry with himself. Angry with his life choices. Angry with what was happening in the here and now.

Mick piloted the boat out into the middle of the river, which Red thought was a mistake. If something happened, they'd be hard-pressed to swim to shore.

Red tried to watch the shadow and the shore at the same time, angling himself on the boat to see everything, if possible.

"Slow down," Karen shouted. "You'll crash into it."

Mick slowed, turning the boat toward the shore slightly. Allowing everyone to see what they were chasing was merely a large school of baitfish in the river.

"False alarm," Fuji said. He pointed to the cruise ship. "Head that way."

Red was smiling. He was glad they'd wasted precious time because of Karen. Even if it meant not getting the footage he wanted. He needed it. Now that Red and Derek didn't work for Easdale, they could sell the footage to the highest bidder. Let Easdale hire a lawyer to sue them for using the station's equipment. He was too cheap to do that.

Two Coast Guard boats were arriving near the cruise ship. Red wondered if there were people in the river. That wouldn't be good.

"Where should I go?" Mick asked.

Red knew his opinion didn't matter so he kept his mouth shut. He focused on watching the area for anything out of the ordinary.

"Closer to the ship," Hunter said. "But go slowly. We need a lot of footage. Angle so we can see those on the docks as well."

As Mick moved the boat into position, Red noticed Karen was staring at him.

"What?" Red finally asked. He was in no mood to deal with a snarky comment or anything she had to say.

Karen moved closer to Red. "I was thinking…"

"Here we go," Red said and shook his head. He'd dealt with Karen Venzi enough times over the years to know this was going to be something ludicrous.

Karen smiled. "Maybe after all of this is done, we can go out for some coffee. Maybe lunch or dinner?"

"Why would you want that?" Red asked.

Karen shrugged her shoulders. "I know we've had our problems. Working for rival news stations, aiming for the same story. The same exclusives. I get it. I am the enemy. But… I like you."

Red felt his face grow hot. "Meaning what?"

"Look, I overheard you with your editor. I know you and Derek quit. I could always use an assistant and a main cameraman. Think about it," Karen said and smiled. "This would be a step up for both of you. I know my bosses will pay you generously, and with me to guide you both, I'll make sure you are mentored properly and can move up in the company. How does that sound?"

To Red it sounded both insulting and like a good deal. He could use the job and the money. He knew Karen would actually help him so she could brag forever how she took this nobody and made him a star.

He wondered what else she wanted. Maybe Karen was into him. Maybe she wanted to make this a romantic coffee, lunch or dinner. Maybe…

"I'll think about it," Red said, trying to act cool.

"Yeah, me too." Derek smiled at Red like he was following his lead.

"Don't think about it too long. With the footage we can both get from all of this, we might be able to flip it to a national news channel by this evening," Karen said. "Legally, I'll need to use their footage for my channel but with the footage you're shooting we can sell it to the highest bidder."

Now Red understood what was happening. Karen was making them believe she was in their corner, was offering a legitimate job, and all she wanted in return was their footage shot so she could make a lot of money off of it.

Red turned away and stood next to Mick. He was done with her games. There was never going to be a romance or a partnership.

As soon as she was able to sell what they had, she would turn her back on Red and Derek. Leave them in her dust.

Red was fuming now. He wanted to tell her off but knew that would be very unprofessional. Especially with Hunter and his team in the boat.

Fuji screamed and Red looked over in time to see something massive rising from out of the water at the bow of the boat.

CHAPTER EIGHTEEN

Red felt the boat rise underneath him a second later, as the monster's head was out of the water but his body was below the boat one second and pitching them sideways the next.

Everyone screamed as the boat flipped, and Red managed to hold his breath as he plunged into the St. Johns River and tried to figure out which way was up so he could swim for air.

The current was strong and Red was swept away, the water threatening to keep him under and drown him.

Red pumped his arms and legs feverishly, in such a panic he wasn't able to see where he was going. He was going to drown. Maybe the St. Johns River Monster was going to eat his dead, limp body as a snack later.

Relax, bro. Stop fighting it, Red thought. He stopped kicking and punching and let his body settle for a couple of seconds. He was still holding his breath but was at the end of his capacity and knew he needed to find the surface quickly.

Red let a few bubbles out of his mouth and watched them float down toward his feet. He was upside down.

He spun around in the water, shapes all around him. Hoping he could break the surface and find the boat.

Something latched onto his ankle and Red freaked out again, thrashing in the water as he tried to get to the surface and air.

It was Hunter, trying to pull himself up using Red as his springboard.

Red kicked Hunter in the face before he realized it wasn't the St. Johns River Monster trying to drag him to the deep.

He kicked his legs and his head broke the surface. Red took in as much air as he could and tried to stay afloat.

Hunter was swimming toward the overturned boat, his nose bleeding.

"Where is everyone?" Red shouted, but Hunter either didn't hear him or ignored Red after getting kicked in the nose.

Red aimed for shore and hoped for the best. He wasn't a bad swimmer, but the fact a giant monster was in the river with him was freaking him out. His mind was racing and he felt on the verge of panicking and not being able to move.

A scream to his left turned him and he saw Karen and Derek nearby, both fighting against the current and trying to get out of the water.

Red needed to get to Derek and help him, but he was worried he couldn't help himself.

Karen had stopped swimming and was staying afloat with her arms, looking down below her feet. "I see it. Oh, dear God, I see it. Right below us."

"Move," Red yelled, and turned to get out of the water as well. He knew they could only swim so fast, and the St. Johns River Monster was definitely faster and more agile in the water. It would only be a matter of time before…

Taco was fifty feet ahead of Red, nearly to the shore, when he rose up and out of the water like he'd been lifted by God and the Rapture was taking him to Heaven, or an alien spaceship, invisible, was in the sky and beaming Taco up for experiments.

It was the creature. The mouth on the pinkish monstrosity had Taco, sharp jagged teeth shredding Taco's torso like a hot knife through butter.

Taco was screaming but Red could already see he'd lost so much blood.

The monster rose into the air, its long pink neck undulating as it began to swallow the chunks of what remained of Taco.

All was chaos as Red tried to swim again, the water around him churning as the creature dove back down under the surface and large waves rippled from the spot it had surfaced to snatch Taco.

Red hadn't said too many words to the man, if any, but it was a gut punch to see someone die so brutally right in front of you.

The water was tinged in blood but only briefly, a wave dissipating the blood.

Karen was ahead of Red now, and she was pumping her arms and legs like she was an Olympic swimmer going for gold.

A few seconds later, she stopped and bobbed in the water.

"What? Keep moving," Red yelled to her.

Karen was shaking her head. She spun back to Red, her eyes huge. "It's right in front of me. Right there." She began to babble and Red could see her eyes glaze over.

She was in shock.

Red wanted to help her. Save her. He paddled toward Karen but when he saw the ripple in the water between her and the shore, he stopped moving. Treaded water.

Was the monster trying to keep them away from safety, herding them? It looked like it.

Red saw with dismay no one had escaped yet. He could see Hunter and Fuji in the distance. Bikini and Lester were closer to him but upriver a bit.

Mick and Derek were next to one another. Close to Karen.

Everyone had paired up for some reason, as if there was safety in numbers. As if the monster wouldn't kill two of them at once, or even attempt it.

Red tried to shake out of it, knowing more of them were going to die. He didn't want to be in that category, and he decided he'd get to safety and help as many of them as he could.

But what if it meant my life? I'm no hero. I can't sacrifice myself for anyone because I'm a coward, Red thought.

He decided to help Karen because she was closer, not because he had a thing for her. Not because he was focusing on her red lips. He was doing that because it distracted him from the imminent death swimming below his exposed feet.

Red looked up when he heard a whirring and saw two news choppers overhead.

"Help us, dammit," Red yelled, knowing it was futile. They weren't there to rescue anyone, they were there to get excellent footage even now they were pumping live on a breaking news story. He wasn't surprised to see his own station – former station – above him. Likely making Easdale happy to see his recently fired employee in so much trouble. So much drama.

Karen was definitely in shock. She was doggy-paddling in a circle, unaware what she needed to do to stay alive.

"Come on, we need to head for shore," Red said and hooked her left arm. He could smell her perfume mixed with the river water and it was both exciting and made him nauseous.

I need to remain focused. I need to live and help Karen, he thought.

Red started to swim and drag her along, but Karen had gone dead weight now.

She was staring toward Bikini and Lester, and Red looked in that direction, too.

The water was parting on the surface as the creature moved, gaining speed, as it shot past Karen and Red and headed straight toward the other two men.

He wanted to scream and tell them to look out, but his lips were dry despite the water splashing into his face.

Karen tensed in his grip and went under, nearly pulling Red with her.

CHAPTER NINETEEN

Red was sucked under and had to push away from Karen so he didn't drown. He watched her spiral down, not even fighting it, her eyes still wide and her mouth open. Was she trying to drown, to kill herself, hoping the creature wouldn't rip her apart while she was alive?

He couldn't concern himself just yet. He broke the surface again and filled his lungs with air before diving back down to rescue her. The silt was kicked up and it was hard to see her. There was a brief glimpse before the water stirred and Red feared the creature was about to attack him.

It was only Karen, finally realizing she was going to die if she didn't help herself. She was kicking her feet and rising past Red like she'd been shot out of a cannon.

He turned back, his rescuing aborted, and met her above water.

"Are you good?" Red asked her.

She actually smiled. "I am. Better. I want to live."

"Yeah, so do I." Red turned to gauge how far from the shore they were. They'd drifted even further away and were in the middle of the river channel now.

Everyone else was equally farther away, drifting apart.

Red started to swim toward shore when he saw the movement in the water ahead, a big dark shape moving so fast from left to right it was nearly a blur.

Like a hammerhead shark, moving in for the kill, Red thought. He loved watching shows about sharks, and Shark Week was his jam.

The St. Johns River Monster was about to attack, and Red turned to see Bikini and Lester were both in the path.

They were too far away to shout and warn them, but Red tried anyway.

Neither man heard the call, and the choppers were still overhead and making so much noise and stirring up the water he didn't think Karen, a few feet away from him, would be able to hear his shout.

Red thought this was a good window for them to escape, while the creature was fixed on attacking someone else. He knew it was an awful thing to think, but someone needed to survive. He was going to do his best to be one of the survivors.

He kept swimming, his arms and legs heavy. He wondered if he had the strength to make it.

It didn't look like it was all that far, but with the fear of getting torn in half at any moment, worrying about Karen and the others, and adrenaline turning to tiredness, safety felt like a thousand miles away.

The current was getting stronger by the minute, and the choppers overhead were churning the water and making it harder to keep moving.

Red saw the shore ahead but it kept moving as he was slowly dragged by the current. He was swimming parallel and had to not only fight to stay afloat, but try to move an inch at a time toward the small beach.

Another fifty yards and his only option would be underneath the bridge itself, because the port, where the big container ships docked and unloaded, was too steep to climb up. At that point he'd need to let the current sweep him away so he could conserve his energy, and pray he wasn't eventually swept all the way downriver and into the Atlantic Ocean.

Karen screamed and Red turned back to see the St. Johns River Monster had resurfaced, its mottled pink hide shaking off water as it moved so quickly, cutting through the water.

The creature was aiming for Bikini or Lester. There was no doubt. Was it going to kill and eat all of them?

"We need to keep moving," Red shouted to Karen. She heard because she nodded and started to swim again.

Red didn't want to watch either of the men being killed, but he couldn't help it. He was still trying to aim for the shore and not get pulled out too far, but he kept turning his head so he could see.

Plus, once the monster was done eating one of the men, he wanted to know where it was heading next. The worst fear was not knowing where it was. If it was underneath and shooting through the water like a Great White shark and he was a seal.

Bikini was lifted into the air by the massive head and jaws of the beast, only a few feet, before the two halves of his body fell to the water below.

The man had died so quickly Red thought he still had a look of confusion on his face, even from this distance.

Both parts of what remained of Bikini started to sink, and the monster turned its head back and forth and swallowed what was left of the man.

Like Bikini was nothing more than a snack or a tasty morsel.

Again, Red hardly knew the man, but it was still tragic and something that would haunt him. If he lived to be haunted, of course.

Right now it doesn't look good for any of us, Red thought.

If the boat had capsized closer to shore maybe they could've escaped. He didn't even know where the boat was at this point, either sunk by the monster or already headed toward the open ocean. Where Red felt like he'd end up.

Better than what had happened to Taco and Bikini.

Lester was paddling and making headway toward safety when Red saw the St. Johns River Monster speeding at him.

Another man will die, Red thought, but couldn't look away.

Lester was only twenty feet from the shore but he was too close to the container ships, where there was no way to exit.

Unless… Red noticed a ladder just above the waterline on the side of the massive ship. Apparently Lester had also seen it, because he was lining up to grab it, hand extended as he moved.

The surface rippled again, and Red held his breath as the wave crashed overhead and nearly took him back under.

When he resurfaced, he saw Karen had drifted further away from him.

He also saw Lester with a hand on the bottom rung of the ladder.

Maybe he'll be the first of many to make it, Red thought.

He was definitely rooting for Lester, who had a second hand on the ladder and was pulling himself up.

The monster did a pass, splashing water onto Lester, who froze on the ladder.

Maybe he'd be able to climb up quickly once the creature has turned to circle back, Red thought.

Lester watched the creature pass before reaching up for the next rung, closer to freedom.

The St. Johns River Monster turned on a dime, underneath the ladder in seconds.

"Climb, climb," Red yelled, more for himself than Lester, who wouldn't be able to hear him.

Lester got two more rungs, only three to go to the top, when the St. Johns River Monster's head reared up.

Even with Lester's torso.

Lester screamed and nearly fell, slipping one hand off of the wet ladder.

Red thought the man would have a better chance, maybe an extra second or two to live, if he fell back into the river and tried to swim for it.

No matter what, Lester was next and the man was a goner.

Lester kicked out, trying to scare or force the creature away.

It did not work, as the monster bit Lester's legs with such force he bent the metal side of the boat, his teeth tearing a chunk of it away and opening the first layer, peeling it back like it was made of paper.

Lester screamed and fell off of the ladder, what was left of him, but his body never got to the water.

The creature was lightning quick and devoured the rest of Lester in the blink of an eye.

Red turned his head and puked into the water.

CHAPTER TWENTY

Hunter had been watching from a distance as he slowly moved through the water, not wanting to panic and splash too much.

It was the old adage: you don't have to outrun the bear, you have to outrun everyone else so the bear is distracted enough to not get you.

He knew it might be construed as cowardly, but he didn't care right now. Survival of the fittest was his only thought, and he was the star here. If he didn't survive, who would be able to tell the story, the real one?

Hunter was still alive because of his strong will to live. He needed to get through anything and everything, and live to tell the tale for paying customers.

"I'm the one who needs to live," he said under his breath over and over, his mantra.

Chupacabra, Bigfoot, aliens, shape-shifters, river and sea monsters, cannibalistic cryptids living underground or in the deep jungles… it didn't matter to Hunter. He'd live to tell the world about what he'd seen and experienced.

While other cryptid and paranormal shows created false narratives and showed fake monsters with smoke and mirrors, Hunter had shown the world what was really out there. Mostly.

True, he'd had to use CGI on a few episodes because they'd never captured anything legitimate on film. He knew the creature was out there because he had a sixth sense for these things, but there was only so much time to search and only so much money to use to film.

Corners were cut not because he wanted to be noticed and even more famous, but because he needed his viewers to know the truth.

Monsters, things that went bump in the night, were real and they were going to kill you.

He watched Fuji struggling in the water and made sure the St. Johns River Monster wasn't in the nearby vicinity before he reached out a hand and helped Fuji to the side of the river.

The big man was too big to be dragged from the water, but Fuji managed like a hurt seal to pop up and out.

"Who has a camera on it?" Hunter asked Fuji, who was breathing heavily. He hoped the big man didn't have a heart attack.

"The idiots above us," Fuji said and pointed at the choppers.

Hunter put up both middle fingers, hoping he was being filmed and they couldn't use the footage or they'd miss something. This footage was too good to be used for free on some local news show. He needed it for a couple of special episodes on his show.

The true believers needed to see this, not a bunch of out of work Jacksonville nobodies or bored housewives doing their husband's laundry.

Real viewers, who believed in Hunter and his journalistic integrity, who wanted to know the unfiltered truth about the corners of the world the governments and the gatekeepers were hiding from everyone.

Hunter knew most of the conspiracies had some level of truth to them. Most cryptids existed or had at some point existed. The natives in all parts of the world had seen them, had lived it, and didn't try to hide the facts. There were no judgements in the old days. Only a collective consciousness. Only the absolute truth.

Hunter looked around. He was on a small pocket of sand that had washed up over many decades, a safe haven. Climbing up and out of it was going to be a hassle. He'd need help, which he didn't want to ask for, even if he could. Better to figure it out himself, rather than be rescued and be at the mercy of looking weak.

"Look," Fuji said.

Hunter at first didn't know what Fuji was pointing at, but he saw it was the boat captain. Mike? Mick? He couldn't remember.

The man was still far out in the river, bobbing on the surface. He'd stopped fighting the current and was drifting along, like he was having a good, leisurely trip. All he was missing was an inner tube.

In seconds, the man was missing his upper body, as the St. Johns River Monster exploded from underneath, turned his long neck and bit the boat captain's uppermost body off.

"Jeez," Hunter exclaimed. The sight was brutal. The monster went back under and the lower body bobbed up and down twice before the creature was back to finish the meal, diving back underwater.

One second the man was there and the next he was gone. There wasn't even blood that Hunter could see, it had been over so quick.

"This is insane. I think I need other, safer work," Fuji said.

"No way. You and I are the only ones remaining. We need a new, better crew. We need to up our game, especially now that we're part of this," Hunter said.

"Can we discuss this after we're rescued? It seems…" Fuji stared at Hunter. "Disrespectful."

Hunter shrugged. "Such is life. I'm sure Taco, Bikini and Lester would want us to go on. Tell their story. Avenge them."

"Avenge them? Are we going to kill the monster?" Fuji asked.

"Metaphorically we will. By airing an episode, maybe a trio of them, about their lives and all they've done and gone through before their early demise." Hunter smiled. He could see a few awards from this, even if they no longer had any actual footage they'd shot. He was sure the idiots in the news choppers were streaming live so he could grab some of it to use.

Hunter was about to tell Fuji everything was going to work out, it always did, and they'd be heroes after all of this, when he spotted the news chick trying to swim for shore. She was too far away for Hunter to rescue her, but he waved his arms as if he was trying to help. Maybe they'd get overhead footage of him trying to help.

"She's not gonna make it," Fuji said, shaking his head. "And she's too far out to swim and rescue."

Hunter knew if she was only five feet away, he still wouldn't chance it. The St. Johns River Monster was really fast and agile in the water. He didn't want to know if it could cruise out of the water and eat them, too, and he wasn't going to get its attention to find out.

Karen bobbed underneath the surface for a second and Hunter was about to call her gone, but then he saw her again. She was still swimming, making way too much noise and splashing too much.

He was about to open his mouth and tell Fuji how he wished he'd gotten the chance to bed the hot chick, but decided Fuji would reprimand him again.

Hunter knew if the woman actually survived, he'd have his shot then. She'd be broken and frail, trying to cope with what had happened. He'd be the strong arm to wrap around her, the shoulder to cry on, the man to sleep with so she could feel better about the world.

He was thinking of some cool lines to use on her to set it up when he saw the wave cresting toward her.

She turned and looked in his direction. Hunter reached out an arm, as if he could save her from this great distance, hoping the cameras in the choppers were rolling on both of them. This would be the perfect footage to use as an opening for the episode.

Karen rose from the water like the Lady in the Lake, the King Arthur myth he'd tried to search for in season three, episode seven of his show.

The St. Johns River Monster had her in his mouth, holding her up like she was a toy.

Karen screamed as the creature bit into her body, folding her in half with its jaws, and Hunter watched her slip down its long throat.

The last thing to disappear was her butt.
Hunter didn't think he'd ever forget that image.

CHAPTER TWENTY-ONE

Red saw Karen die and stopped swimming. Past where she'd been a second ago was only a swirl of water as the creature went back under.

Further away was Hunter and Fuji, safe on a small strip of beach. Red knew the St. Johns River Monster could grab both of them in a heartbeat if it wanted to.

He turned and looked for Mick. He thought he might be the only one alive still in the water, and Red wanted to cry.

Was everyone really dead, except Hunter, Fuji and himself? So many deaths in such a short time, all being recorded from above.

He saw a shadow and looked down to see the creature swimming underneath him.

Red tried not to panic but he started to swim, as if his life depended on it. Which it surely did.

As the creature made another quick pass like a shark, Red noticed something gleaming on the back of the beast.

Red dipped his head underwater to get a better view.

It was a harpoon jabbed into the creature's side, the thick rope severed, trailing behind.

The monster had been attacked at some point and still had the harpoon embedded in its thick hide.

I can do this, Red thought. *This is the only chance we have.*

He stopped swimming to conserve his strength, knowing if the next pass was the attack, there was nothing he could do. The teeth of the creature were like steak knives, two tight rows of them. Red imagined the jaw had enough strength to crush his limbs with ease.

Based on how easy it was for the monster to tear everyone else in half, Red knew he might have one shot in a million to make this work.

Red watched as the creature did another pass, which was great for Red. He held his breath and dove down, hoping the creature wasn't too fast for him.

The St. Johns River Monster slowed, turning to reach Red, who nearly panicked and let his held breath go.

Red was able to swim down, past the snapping jaws, and slide down the side of the creature.

This close, it was even bigger than he'd thought. He didn't know if he could hold his breath long enough to do the crazy thing he was going to try.

Red reached for the harpoon but the creature swung around and swiped Red with his massive tail, knocking the wind from Red.

He sputtered to the surface, coughing and close to drowning.

The monster swam past him, inches away with a good angle to bite Red in half easily.

Is it toying with me now? Because I'm the last one in the water? It's trying to intimidate me, as if it needs to, Red thought.

He got his bearings and watched as the St. Johns River Monster passed by again, far below the surface. Red figured it was going to come up fast and strike, and there was no way he'd be able to get out of the way.

Red braced for another pass, hoping it wasn't with an open mouth filled with teeth.

The St. Johns River Monster circled around underneath before shooting away, toward where Hunter and Fuji were standing.

"Here he comes," Red yelled, but he was too far away for the pair to hear him.

Red started to swim toward shore but not too fast. He didn't want the creature to hear his splashing and turn back to investigate.

He got a few feet before he saw the head rise above the water, headed back at him.

This is it. Make a stand, no matter how weak it is, Red thought.

He was going to die but not go down without a fight. Even if it didn't even annoy the monster. Better than to simply get eaten.

Instead of a direct assault, the creature went past Red and immediately started to turn, like it was getting behind him.

That was all Red needed, another chance. He dove down and the jaws took a chomp out of the water inches from his face. He could feel the vacuum of it because the creature was so big.

He swam down to the side he'd seen the harpoon and took hold of it as the monster started to swim away.

Red held on for dear life as the St. Johns River Monster sped up, obviously feeling Red hanging on for a ride.

The St. Johns River Monster was moving so fast Red didn't have time to do anything but hold on with both hands, hoping the harpoon eventually pulled free when he was near the surface so he had a fighting chance of getting air.

The monster thrashed back and forth to shake him, but Red held on. As the creature turned, Red felt the harpoon dig deeper into the side of it. Blood was seeping into the water, giving it a light tint when the monster stopped.

Red lifted up, still gripping the harpoon, and his head broke the surface of the water.

The St. Johns River Monster had its head above water as well, looking down its massive neck at Red.

Teeth dropped water and Red could see bits of flesh between the teeth.

"Let's do this," Red said, taking a deep breath and ducking under the surface. If the creature wanted Red, it would need to come and get him.

He wrapped his arms around the harpoon and decided to push it in further if he could get the proper grip. He put both feet on the creature's thick skin and leaned onto the harpoon, using his weight to push it in deeper.

It worked, because the creature started to buck, tossing Red off of it.

Red went under briefly but came back up and treaded water as the St. Johns River Monster thrashed around on the surface.

The harpoon must've hit something vital because as the monster flipped out, more and more blood was being pumped from the wound and into the water.

Red could smell the coppery blood and was covered in it.

The St. Johns River Monster dove under and the surface of the river began to settle again.

Red swam for shore.

He was getting closer to Hunter and Fuji when he saw both men look up with fear in their eyes.

Red knew the monster was still alive and right behind him, the waves pushing him forward now.

Red knew better than to turn around. He pumped his arms and legs as fast as he could with what little strength he had.

Finally getting to the strip of beach, Red collapsed on the sand and rolled onto his back, waiting for certain death.

The St. Johns River Monster reared up from the water, fifteen feet in the air, its mouth opened wide, showing its teeth.

Red, Hunter and Fuji screamed. There was nothing they could do to defend themselves. The creature could pick them off one at a time.

"It's bleeding badly," Red shouted, pointing at the wound.

The harpoon was even deeper than Red thought he'd shoved it, and the blood was pumping out as the monster moved. It looked sluggish and its head rolled on the long neck, as if it was trying to keep it up.

Hunter was behind Red, and when Red moved to his left he knew Hunter was moving with him, like Red was a human shield.

If one of us dies, all three of us will, Red thought. Once the monster struck, it would keep attacking until they were all dead.

The St. Johns River Monster began to lower its head, teeth gleaming, when the eyes rolled back in the head and the neck came down, nearly hitting Red.

It took its last breath.

Hunter pushed Red away and put a foot on the neck of the monster, smiling and looking up at the choppers.

"This is the money shot, boys," Hunter said. "I'll be on every cover of every magazine. Footage on every news program."

Red groaned. "You didn't do anything."

Hunter glanced at Red and winked. "Perception, Red. The picture is worth a thousand words."

Fuji laughed, shaking his head.

CHAPTER TWENTY-TWO

The press conference was huge and made Red uncomfortable. An interim governor was there, on the JAXPORT docks, shaking hands and telling the survivors how brave they were. What an honor it was to meet them. Another half dozen soundbytes in front of the rolling cameras.

There were pictures taken and short interviews, looking for the important things said. The clips they could shoot out on every news program.

Hunter Shaya with his foot defiantly on the neck of the St. Johns River Monster. A smile on his face, and knowing look like he single-handedly defeated the cryptid.

Like he saved not only the good citizens of Jacksonville but the world.

A passing mention was made about all those lost during the attacks, a frown and silent nod from everyone. Families would be left to grieve in private. The names of the dead would be published, short clips about the wonderful people from family, friends and old high school classmates. Everyone had died a saint, their losses making the world infinitely darker on the other side.

Red had cried for hours afterward, once the adrenaline rush was gone. Once Mick's body, what little was left of it, washed ashore. His best friend was dead. Because Red had included him in this awful adventure. Why had he even been a part of this?

He wondered if he'd have been better off staying at home, working as a gopher and shuffling people back and forth from the airport.

Easdale had left a message, asking Red to call him. When he had, Easdale asked where his last paycheck and his items he'd left at the office should be mailed to. As if he didn't already have the information.

Red wondered if his former boss was looking for an apology. Likely he wanted Red to beg for his old job back, as if it meant that much anymore to Red.

Derek was in the same spot, having also lost his job. He seemed happier about it, though.

"What are you going to do now?" Red asked him. The two were standing off to the side, away from the press and the lights and the cameras.

Red could only shrug.

Derek was smoking a cigarette. He turned and flicked it into the river behind him. "Maybe we could try to find work as a package deal at another station. Not trying to be morbid or funny, but you might have some weight thanks to your involvement in all of this. Karen Venzi needs replacing, you know?"

Red shrugged again. "The history of this will quickly show I did nothing."

"You're the one who killed the St. Johns River Monster."

"No, Hunter Shaya did. See? He's up there now telling his version of what happened, and they are hanging on his every word," Red said. "The record will show Hunter Shaya hit the monster with his harpoon, the one he brought for just such an event. He stood on the head of the beast and slayed him thusly."

Derek laughed. "Yeah, you're probably right."

As the crowd cheered, Red wanted to run away. Hide. Do not think about any of this. He'd dried off but he still felt wet. He needed a shower and a change of clothing.

"Hey, wanna get out of here and go get a beer or ten and get drunk?" Derek asked.

Red thought about it for a second and smiled. "Yeah, I do."

They walked through the crowd as another cheer went up.

Red and Derek didn't have their phones anymore, so they'd need to figure out how to order an Uber. Maybe they could find someone in the crowd who'd offer a lift.

"Hey, Red. Derek. Wait up."

Red turned to see Fuji approaching. "Where are you going? Hunter said he was going to pull you onstage with him."

"I'm not interested," Red said.

Derek didn't even bother to answer.

"Where are you headed?" Fuji asked. "Hopefully the nearest bar."

Red nodded. "I'd just as soon forget all of this."

"Wait for me and Hunter. We'll go, too. I know he wanted to see you before we flew back north." Fuji waited for an answer.

"Fine. See if he can get us a ride. We left the rental back at the dock," Red said. *Near Mick's dock. Where his pickup truck is still parked.*

Red refused to go closer to the stage, preferring the quiet company of Derek and the parked cars. He wanted to curl up and cry for days. Not even about what had happened to him, but everyone that had been lost. The damage that was done to Jacksonville.

Cry about Mick and the lost friendship. How hard he'd been on his friend at times. How impatient Red had been as well.

The crowd started to disperse and Red got out of the way.

A few minutes later, Hunter and Fuji arrived, both sharing a joke.

"Where are we going for beers, Red? I say back to TacoLu's. I liked that place, and it's far enough away we might be able to drink and eat in peace," Hunter said.

They got a ride to the mini-van and Red drove them to TacoLu's, where they were welcomed back like returning heroes and given a prime space at the bar. A few people came over and congratulated them, mostly Hunter, and several rounds of drinks and shots were purchased for the four of them.

"What are you going to do now, Red?" Hunter asked.

Red smiled. "That seems to be the question, I guess." He shrugged. "I'm not sure yet. I guess I need to find a job somewhere in town."

Fuji was smiling at Red. "Can I ask him, boss?"

"Sure." Hunter downed another tequila shot.

"We want to hire you," Fuji said.

"For what?"

Hunter slapped Red on the back, hard. He was already very drunk. "We have a few openings in our crew. Not that I need to remind you. How would you like to work for me? Travel around the world. Search for terrifying monsters. Hit on beautiful local women. Every week for the rest of your life, or until my ratings slip far enough down I'm canceled."

Red was about to dismiss the invite immediately, but instead he took another sip of his beer. Would he be able to leave Jacksonville, where he'd grown up? Everything he knew was right here.

But… What was even left in Jacksonville for him? Mick was gone. He didn't have a job. His apartment was shabby and he never made great money. There were no love interests, no women who he thought would give him the time of day.

"I could be a nobody here for the rest of my life, or do it all over the world," Red said and smiled. "Yes."

Hunter smiled and slapped him hard again. "Perfect."

Derek looked uncomfortable next to Red.

"What about you, cameraman? We could use your skills." Hunter grinned. "Even though your camera is at the bottom of the river."

"It wasn't my camera. The news channel I used to work for will have to go fish it out," Derek said. "I'd love to see the world."

"Then we'll fly back to New York and you two get your affairs in order," Hunter said. "I'll get plane tickets and work out the salaries, too. Give me a week or so and then we'll begin."

"All of the footage we have already that's been public will need to be combed through," Fuji said. "Create a narrative for a few episodes. The channel we work for is super excited to do a special two-parter about this."

"Of course, the two of you will be interviewed as survivors and paid accordingly," Hunter said. He pointed at Derek. "From now on, we'll call you D-Train."

"Okay," Derek – now D-Train – said.

"What about me?"

Hunter grinned again. "Red. You're always going to be Red, man."

"How come you don't have a nickname?" Red asked Hunter.

Fuji chuckled.

"Do you think my parents named me Hunter? Jeez. My real name is Kevin, but keep that to yourself."

CHAPTER TWENTY-THREE

"Look, Mama, the rocks are pink," Lucille said as she walked the beach.

Her mother frowned. "I don't think they're rocks. Leave them alone and come back over and play so I can see you."

Lucille looked back to the beach and saw her mother wasn't even looking over at her. She had those thick white sunglasses she wore, thinking she looked hip and edgy.

At seven, Lucille knew more about hip and edgy than her mama did. She spent a lot of time after school each day on YouTube watching fashion videos.

Her papa was snoring loudly on the beach blanket nearby, his back bright red from not using suntan lotion.

Lucille went back to looking at the pretty rocks.

There were four of them and they were wedged in the small jetty of rocks jutting into the Amelia River. She knew that was the name of it because there were a few signs on the beach and her papa was telling them a lot of stupid history about the area, talking about pirate ships and lost treasure and whatnot.

None of that interested Lucille. That was for dumb boys. She wanted to know about what the women had worn back in those days, especially the shoes. Lucille already had what her mama called an unhealthy obsession with footwear.

This vacation was supposed to be fun, but so far Lucille was bored. When she'd heard they were coming to Florida, she imagined Disney and amusement park rides. Going shopping for summer clothes you couldn't find in stupid, boring Wisconsin.

They were staying in Amelia Island, which had a lot of clothing stores, but her parents weren't interested in going into any of them except to buy cheap t-shirts with Amelia Island on them. They ate a lot of food so far and her parents both drank way too much alcohol. During the daytime, too.

Lucille had never seen either of her parents drinking. Not that she could remember.

Even the beach they were at was lame. It was small and part of a state park. There weren't any other people on it, especially children to play with.

Her papa had explained to them a few times how they could swim across the river and be in Georgia, that was how close they were.

Papa had said it enough her mama asked him to please stop with the history lessons so she could read her new paperback book.

Even her book looked boring, with a boat on the horizon and the sun going down. Maybe it was coming up. Lucille didn't know and didn't care. All she knew was it had to be an adult book her mama would hide from her, as if she was going to read it.

Lucille wanted to pick the pretty pink rocks up and look at them closer, but knew her mama would yell if she saw her touch them.

Another glance back and Lucille saw her mama was back to reading her book, digging her feet in the sand.

"Just a quick look," Lucille thought. "What will that harm?"

As soon as she picked the first one up, she felt the heat emanating from it. Prickly heat against her fingertips. Not too hot she couldn't hold it, but enough she knew not to put it in her palm and close her fingers around it.

The heat was exciting. She'd never felt a rock that was hot. Once she'd picked up a potato wrapped in tinfoil on a plate and burned her hand, but that was when she was a little, little kid in kindergarten.

She remembered Mama had started to freak out but Papa shrugged and said that was a good way to learn not to touch things you're not supposed to touch.

It was a lesson Lucille still hadn't learned.

The rock didn't feel as heavy as a normal rock. She shook it and thought she heard and felt it move inside, like it was hollow or had room in it.

Lucille smiled. What if it was a bird? It could be a flamingo. They were pink, right?

"What are you doing, honey?" her mama yelled.

"Nothing," Lucille said and turned, dropping the rock behind her. She knew if she was caught she'd be grounded, and then this lame vacation would be even lamer. "Why?"

"Come and get something to drink. I need to put more lotion on you," her mama said. "Unlike your father, who's going to be crying like a baby tonight."

In reply, her papa snored louder.

Lucille got a bottle of water and sat on the sand while her mama rubbed lotion in.

"I saw some pretty pink rocks," Lucille told her mama, as if she hadn't already mentioned it. "They looked hot."

Her mama chuckled. "Because we're in Florida, honey. Everything is going to be hot. Don't touch anything. There might be germs and viruses on the rocks we don't have in Wisconsin. You don't want to mix them or you'll get sick."

Lucille didn't think that was the way it worked. She might only be a kid but she didn't think different germs and viruses were waiting on rocks in Florida for someone from Wisconsin to touch them and unleash a deadly plague.

Something was moving in the sand near where the rocks were.

"I won't touch them," Lucille lied. She wanted to see if all of them were hot. Maybe that first one was because of the sun beating down on it.

Lucille picked up another two rocks, both of them hot.

There were two more pink rocks and Lucille picked them up, too. They were too big for her little hands and she had to finally pick one from each hand, dropping the others back on the sand.

One of the rocks split on the side.

Lucille bent down to see what was inside and grinned when she saw there was a small creature. It was pink and looked like a dragon. Not a flamingo, if she remembered correctly what they looked like.

She bent down to get a closer look. It was moving, which delighted her.

One of the other rocks was also cracked and she could see a small creature inside of it, too.

"Honey, come back over here," her mama yelled.

"Okay, just a second." Lucille stood but didn't move. She watched as both creatures broke through the shells – not rocks – and started to crawl slowly.

"Mama, come see what I found. They're alive."

"Honey, stay away from wild animals. That's how you get hurt."

Lucille bent back down. "No, Mama, they're so little and cute. Maybe squishy." She reached out her hand and put it near one of them.

The closest one shot away from her and headed into the water, disappearing.

Lucille was sad until she saw the other creature was still in front of her, inches from her fingers.

"Come and look, Mama. They're so cute and–"

It had teeth, which it sunk into her pinkie.

Lucille cried out and stood, but the creature held on, sinking teeth deeper into her finger.

"Honey, come over here right now," her mama was yelling.

Lucille panicked. "It won't leave me alone. It's hurting me."

Her papa was up in seconds, rushing at her while her mama stayed in her chair.

"What the… stop moving, honey," her papa said and put his own fingers around the creature, squeezing it until the thing finally released its grip on her pinkie with a plop sound.

Her papa had crushed it between his fingers and flicked it away.

"Let me see," he said.

Lucille held up her bleeding finger. It was throbbing.

"Come on. We need to get you to a hospital. You might have rabies," her papa said.

Lucille knew she didn't have rabies.

She glanced back to see the other shells were also now broken, and the creatures were making their way to Amelia River.

The End